Satisfied

"Excuse me, ma'am, do you want your oil checked?"

Holly forced her eyes away from the vending machines and back to the attendant. "Huh?" she said.

"The oil?" he asked again.

Holly looked at him for the first time. He was good-looking in a dark, rough-edged way. Here, at least, was one guy whose attention wasn't fixed on the blonde. She started to say no. Then she was inspired, remembering Fiona's words about giving Bart a dose of his own medicine. One quick look out of the corner of her eye, and she satisfied herself: Bart was still ogling the blonde, who seemed to be taking a very long time fixing her tire. Holly slipped her glasses on top of her head, and looked straight into the guy's dark brown eyes. "The oil's okay, but could you be a sweetheart and check the wiper fluid? No one's checked it in ages." She leaned out of the car window and smiled at him invitingly.

Books from Scholastic
in the **Couples** series:

COUPLES

BE MINE!

by M.E. Cooper

SCHOLASTIC INC.
New York Toronto London Auckland Sydney

ISBN 0-590-40423-7

12 11 10 9 8 7 6 5 4 3 2 1   7 8 9/8 0 1 2/9

Printed in the U.S.A.   01

First Scholastic printing, January 1987

Chapter

1

Bart Einerson pulled his Jeep over to the curb. He turned off the headlights but left the engine idling. A big full moon hung low over the road and seemed to fill the windshield. "You still have time to change your mind," he said, turning to face Holly Daniels. She sat in the passenger seat looking at the long line of cars parked from Jonathan Preston's driveway clear down to the corner of the street. Holly had turned up the collar of her pea coat against the cold, and Bart couldn't make out her expression in the dark. "Holly," he coaxed, reaching across the seat and touching her shoulder, "we can always pretend we couldn't find a parking place."

Holly gave a little laugh and took Bart's hand in hers. As she turned toward him, the moonlight lit up her pretty face. Holly's cheeks were pink from the cold and matched her beret. Bart smiled slowly and gently touched the tip of her nose: It was peeling slightly from the sunburn she'd gotten skiing with him the weekend before. A familiar feeling of warmth shot through her. When Bart looked at her that way, she could barely resist him — even when he was making dumb suggestions like he was now. She playfully pushed his hand away and tried to sound stern. "Everyone's expecting us," Holly said, her breath coming out all frosty. "We're late already. By the time we get to this 'Beat the February Blahs' party, it's going to be March! Why don't you want to go, anyway?"

"I'd just rather be alone with you," Bart whispered, unclicking Holly's seat belt and drawing her toward him. "The party's probably so crowded by now, no one will miss us." He pulled off her fuzzy beret and tossed it in the backseat, where it landed next to his Stetson. He ran his fingers through her short brown curls.

Holly tried to protest, but as he slipped his hands around her slim waist, her big hazel eyes were shining. Holly gave a pleasant little shiver and wrapped her arms around him. He felt so strong and warm. The collar of his letter jacket was scratchy and rough, but the skin on the nape of his neck was incredibly smooth and soft. Holding Bart like this was the most wonderful feeling in the world. She sighed contentedly and pressed her cheek against his chest. His heart was pounding, just like hers.

Holly closed her eyes and tried to remember what her life had been like before Bart, before moving back to Rose Hill in September and starting her junior year at Kennedy High. It had been okay. Not good, not bad, just plain old, ordinary okay. She went to a Baltimore high school twice the size of Kennedy and not half as good. Holly had spent most of her time studying; she was very determined to go to college. She had had a few good friends, and now and then she had dated guys in her class. They had been nice, but she hadn't fallen in love with any of them. Bart was the first guy she had ever really loved.

Holly let out a long sigh and let her hands slip around Bart's back. "I just got the craziest thought," she murmured.

"What's that?" His voice was soft, caring.

Holly pushed back slightly, and lifted her face toward his. "I wonder if some places are just more lucky for people than others. . . . Like Rose Hill. I loved it here when I was a kid, and Phoebe and I went to school together. Life seemed so perfect then. Now I'm back, and I love it, and life's perfect again."

Holly didn't have to say more. She knew Bart understood what she meant. When she was twelve her parents got divorced, and she moved with her mother to Baltimore. All Holly really remembered about that time was feeling hurt. She had been convinced her mom and dad split up because of something she'd done. Then slowly, very slowly, Holly had begun to see that the problems between them had nothing to do with her — just like they had both tried to tell her. Since then, her dad had remarried and moved to California. Now her mom had found someone new, too. Very recently she had told

3

Holly she was marrying Bruce Wengar, the pharmacist who owned a drugstore near the Albatross bookstore in town. Their wedding was set for the first day of summer. Yes, Rose Hill was turning into a very wonderful place for Holly and her mom.

Bart's hands tightened around her. "Do you know how much I love you?" he asked softly.

Holly suddenly had the craziest urge to cry. She really couldn't remember ever being this happy. She looked up at Bart, her face beaming. He lowered his lips toward hers. As they kissed, Holly forgot about the party, and being late, and how cold it was inside the beat-up Jeep with the broken heater.

Finally, they relaxed in each other's arms. Holly rested her head against Bart's shoulder while Bart toyed with the delicate jade and silver earring dangling from her right ear. He cleared his throat and said, "I was thinking — it's such a clear night, and the roads are dry, and it's kind of late to turn up at the party. Maybe we could go for a ride . . . up to the hills, west of here. We could look at some of those constellations you're studying. Think of it as a field trip — maybe you could teach me something." Bart grinned at Holly in the dark.

Holly pulled back and gave a low laugh. "I'm not quite sure what you have in mind for me to teach you, but there aren't any stars tonight." She reached into the backseat for her hat and pulled it on. She checked her reflection in the rearview mirror. "There's a moon, Bart," she

4

continued, tapping the windshield for emphasis. "A big, full moon. Very bad for stargazing."

Bart took hold of her hand again and pretended to think. "Why, then, it's our last chance to see these snowy fields in the moonlight. Next full moon will be almost spring."

Holly raised her eyebrows and laughed until Bart silenced her with another kiss. Going to Jonathan's party wasn't exactly what she felt like doing right now, either, even though Kennedy High's popular student activities director was notorious for throwing the greatest parties in town. But Holly had promised Bart's sister Diana that they would turn up after her shift at the Rose Hill medical clinic. The Maryland hills, moonlit snow, and having Bart's arms around her sounded much more appealing. If he asked her again, she might not turn down his offer.

She decided not to give him a chance to ask her one more time. It was a school night, the party would probably break up early, and she had promised her friends she'd be there. Holly slipped her hand out of Bart's, and opened the car door. "Race you!" she challenged over her shoulder and leaped lightly to the ground. She tore down the block, but Bart reached the white picket fence a moment before she did, proving exactly why he was one of Kennedy's star athletes. Bart scooped her into his arms, pushed through the gate, and carried her — laughing and kicking — down the gravel path to Jonathan's front door.

The living-room lights were down comfortably low, and the crowd was gathered in front of the blazing fireplace. Bart was leaning against the mantelpiece, tuning a guitar to notes Michael played on the old upright piano against the stairway wall. The air smelled of popcorn, toasted marshmallows, and Kim Barrie's special cocoa heating in the kitchen. Everyone was waiting for the music to begin, but the silence suited Holly just fine. Tonight she didn't need to talk to anyone. Holly just wanted to enjoy the feeling of being with good friends, and most of her closest friends were here. Bart's sister Diana was curled up on the rug, her blonde head in Jeremy Stone's lap. As usual, Jeremy was chatting briskly in his impeccable British accent, though Holly couldn't tell if he was talking to Diana or Jonathan. Fiona Stone was sitting on the floor, with her back propped against Jonathan's and her nose buried in one of the paperback mysteries Jonathan's mother had written. Jonathan was always teasing his dancer girl friend that she was dating him just to hang out at his house and devour his mother's collection of mystery books. Ted Mason was staring pensively into the fire. Phoebe Hall was next to her boyfriend Michael on the piano bench and Woody Webster was busy tossing popcorn kernels at Sherlock, the Prestons' basset hound. A peal of laughter floated down the hall from the kitchen, where Dee Patterson, Marc Harrison, and Kim Barrie were preparing more munchies.

Holly looked up at Bart and smiled. His

strong body was curved over the guitar, his cheek pressed against the gleaming wood as he tuned it. The fire lit up his rugged features, accenting his prominent cheekbones and square jaw. For the second time that night, she felt like the luckiest girl in the world. Not only was the guy she loved a true friend, but he was so incredibly handsome that sometimes just looking at him took her breath away.

Bart strummed some random chords, then shifted into a familiar progression, and Holly's heart skipped a beat. She recognized the tune before anyone else in the room did. It was her favorite western-style ballad, "Desperado," and Bart sang it to her often. It had become their song. She knew that was why he was playing it now. It was his way of saying across the crowded room that he was wishing they were alone in the Maryland hills, studying the stars.

Holly met his eyes and held his glance as she joined in the chorus, her low voice harmonizing with Bart's strong, melodic baritone.

At the end of the song, Woody Webster led the cheers. "Bless my suspenders, Einerson, you are one talented guy!" Woody pronounced, ignoring Kim's protests and popping the last marshmallow into his mouth. "You should trade in those cowboy boots and your home back there on the range" — Woody gestured vaguely in the direction he believed was west — "for a career in show biz. You'll leave them fainting in the aisles."

"He already has," Fiona reminded Woody in her clipped English accent. "Don't you remember those freshman girls turning up at the *Oklahoma!* cast party with a bunch of roses for our hero?"

Phoebe doubled over with laughter, recalling the scene at Michael's house in December. "I opened the door, and I thought the flowers were for me. Whoever heard of flowers for the leading man?"

"When Bart Einerson's around, *everyone* takes a backseat!" Woody teased.

"Aw, it wasn't such a big deal!" Bart sounded embarrassed but his eyes sparkled. As he stretched out his long legs in front of the fire and rubbed the pointy toe of one intricately worked cowboy boot against the other, he looked very pleased with himself.

Holly smiled and tried to look as proud of Bart as Bart did. But it was hard. She didn't like being reminded of how all the girls at Kennedy seemed to find Bart so attractive.

Michael's next comment didn't help. "Maybe Peter Lacey can tape Bart singing that tune to use as the WKND Candy Hearts theme song."

Holly cringed, then relaxed a little as Bart covered his face with his hands and groaned. "Spare me!" It was no secret that he — and most of the other guys — hated the whole idea of Peter's two-week-long Valentine's advice-to-the-lovelorn feature spot. Candy Hearts had been aired only two days now, and already it was the most listened-to five minutes on the school radio station. Sasha Jenkins, editor of the school paper, had glumly announced in the sub shop that afternoon that even over her protests *The Red and the Gold* staff had voted to pick up Candy Hearts's *Heartache Hotline* as a regular weekly column next year.

"Speaking of Valentine's Day!" Woody jumped to his feet and gave his red suspenders a resounding snap. "It's time for Earthly Delights' big announcement." Woody turned to Michael and said, "Drum roll, please."

While Michael obliged with a fancy chord on the piano, Kim marched into the room carrying a tray heaped with heart-shaped cookies of all sizes. Some were glazed with pink sugar frosting, some had sprinkles, most had candy hearts embedded in their centers.

"What's this?" Jonathan asked. "Valentine's Day isn't for a couple of weeks yet."

"It's the kickoff for my advertising campaign — you're the lucky ones who get to be the test market," Kim explained, passing the tray around. She playfully slapped Woody's hand as he reached for the first cookie. "Woodrow Wilson Webster, you've already had a whole boxful. Be fair," she scolded before continuing. "It's a preview, really. I'm starting a new business for the holiday called 'Sweets to the Sweet.'"

Dee took a very small cookie and asked, "What happened to Earthly Delights?" Kim's mother ran a successful catering business and the crowd's parties always benefited from Kim's considerable culinary skills.

"Nothing. That's Mom's business. This is my own. I'm going to set up a table in the cafeteria to take orders, starting next week. I'm going to take care of the delivery end of the service."

"Great!" Phoebe clapped. "I think it's a terrific idea."

"And the valentines can say anything you want?" Fiona asked, a mischievous glint lighting up her blue eyes.

"You bet," Kim replied. "And I guarantee absolute confidentiality. In other words, this is a good time to let your secret love know your secrets. Sweets to the Sweet won't tell."

"And I won't, either," Woody chimed in, dramatically crossing his heart. "I had to go through top-level security clearance for my end of the job. I'm sworn to utmost secrecy. It's in my contract. If I blab — " Woody drew his long, thin finger across his throat, "It's all over." He dropped to the floor and played dead. Sherlock bounded over and began licking his face. "Hey, don't take it literally." Woody scrambled to his feet and pushed down the affectionate hound. "I don't want to be *your* dinner."

"We could see who gets the most valentines and give them a prize," Jonathan suggested. "You wouldn't have to say *who* the cookies were from, or anything."

Ted raised his eyebrows to the ceiling. "That would be no contest. Everyone knows who'll win that one!"

Diana practically choked on her cookie. "I do." She smothered a laugh and stared in Holly's direction.

Holly looked puzzled. "Laurie Bennington, Chris Austin?" she asked, naming a couple of the most popular and attractive girls in the senior class.

"No way!" Marc laughed. "After school to-day, the pep club announced the winner of their informal 'Most Popular Guy at Kennedy High' contest."

Holly's heart stopped. She didn't have to hear the results to know who the winner was, but she took a deep breath and forced a smile as she said, "Let me guess." She paused for a moment. "Bart Einerson?" Bart took an awkward bow and she applauded gallantly in his direction.

"Gosh, I hope I don't need a wheelbarrow to deliver the goods to Einerson," Woody joked.

"Maybe a van," Ted said.

Bart smiled sheepishly at Holly. His whole expression seemed to say, "Don't blame me, it's not my fault." This time Holly couldn't return his smile. Holly knew it wasn't his fault. Bart couldn't help being cute. She just wished he wouldn't encourage all the attention he received. After all, they were a pretty well-known campus duo by now, but Holly's presence never seemed to faze Bart's admirers. When they first met last fall, Bart, as new to Kennedy as Holly, had already made a name for himself as a first-string defensive lineman on the football team. Maybe it was his unusually rugged good looks, or his ir-resistible smile, but somehow he had attracted an incredible number of groupies. Girls were al-ways phoning him, leaving flowers outside his locker, or taping notes to the windshield of his Jeep. Then, after his stint in *Oklahoma!*, the notes and calls increased. Bart just laughed about it. Holly tried to laugh along, but lately she was having a hard time acting like she didn't care.

11

She felt that Bart should try harder to let his fans know he was involved with someone, instead of encouraging their interest.

Holly was beginning to wish they hadn't come to this party at all. She hadn't had the February blahs until just now. Bart came over to sit beside Holly. He had a pile of cookies and was busy munching them down. Holly had taken one small cookie with a blue candy heart on it. She hadn't taken one bite. "Saving it for me?" Bart whispered, his fingers creeping toward hers. Holly handed him the cookie without protest.

Ted and Marc were still carrying on about Bart. Something about truckloads and freight cars of cookies. Holly didn't feel much like eating, listening to them joke about Bart's popularity. Bart picked the blue candy heart off the top of the cookie and tried to pop it into Holly's mouth. She took it in her hand instead and let out a barely perceptible sigh as she studied the heart. She hadn't seen one of these since she was a kid. ONLY YOU, the tiny letters said. Then she did something she hadn't done since the sixth grade: She popped the candy into her mouth and made a wish that it was true — that she was the only girl in Bart Einerson's life. The thought made the tiny candy ridiculously hard to swallow and Holly had the feeling she was about to cry.

Just then, Phoebe's voice rang out across the room. "You guys are crazy. Nobody's going to get that many cookies. A knapsack is all Woody's going to need to make his deliveries," she said with a sympathetic glance in Holly's direction. . . . But Holly didn't notice.

She didn't want to listen anymore. She jumped to her feet and grabbed an empty popcorn bowl, then mumbled something about refills, and walked out of the dimly lit room and into the fluorescent glare of the kitchen. The dishwasher was humming, and from upstairs a child's high-pitched voice competed with the banging of a typewriter. In the cozy, romantic atmosphere of the living room, Holly had forgotten that this was a weeknight party, and Jonathan's parents were home and still up.

Holly carefully put the bowl on the counter and leaned back against the sink. She threw back her head and stared at the bleak white ceiling. Was going out with Bart always going to be like this? Was she always going to have to sit there and listen to her friends tease him about how many girls he could get if he really wanted them? She was supposed to laugh along with the other kids, pretending to be pleased that Bart didn't want every girl who threw herself at his feet. He only wanted her. Everyone *knew* that. And Holly knew it was true, too. But what would happen if one day some really great girl — someone as terrific as one of her friends, Fiona, or Dee, or Phoebe — gave Bart the eye? What would happen then? Holly's stomach seemed to plummet about a mile. She hugged her arms around herself and tried to swallow the lump in her throat.

"Daniels," she whispered. "You're overreacting."

13

Being voted Kennedy's most popular guy was hardly Bart's fault. But dating Kennedy's most popular guy sometimes felt like walking a tightrope over a dangerous ravine: One wrong step and a million other girls would come leaping off the sidelines to claim Bart as their own. After dating Holly for almost four months now, why did Bart have such a hard time letting other girls know he was taken? The more they threw themselves at him, the more he seemed to flirt back. And he insisted his flirting didn't mean a thing. When they had first started dating, they had talked it out and Bart had told her that. He had also told her he'd try to change. Maybe he had. Maybe he used to flirt more. Holly had no way of knowing what Bart was like in Montana, but she had seen him in action around Rose Hill, where he had become known as the town flirt. The problem was, she didn't know what to do about it. No matter how happy she felt with Bart, there was this constant doubt in her mind. Holly couldn't help herself. She was jealous and being jealous hurt.

One tear, then another, slipped down Holly's cheek. She leaned against the refrigerator door and cried very softly. She was standing like that when Diana walked into the kitchen.

"Holly?" Diana paused in the doorway. She had her down vest over one arm and was carrying a tray of empty soda cans. "What happened?" she asked, closing the kitchen door and hurrying to Holly's side.

Holly sniffed and wiped at her tears. "Nothing. Nothing happened."

14

Diana set down the tray and pushed her long blonde hair off her face. She pulled a couple of tissues out of a box on the counter and handed them to Holly. Then she leaned back and waited for Holly to speak. After a few moments of silence Diana said, "It's Bart, isn't it?"

Holly wiped her eyes. She looked at the tissue and gave an embarrassed little laugh. Crying in front of friends wasn't really her style. "This mascara really is waterproof." She tried to laugh, then bit her lip. Finally she met Diana's deep brown eyes. "Yeah, it's Bart, I guess. I mean nothing happened, it's just — "

"The way Ted was razzing him," Diana finished for Holly. "It was kind of dark in there, but I could tell you were upset."

Holly walked away from the refrigerator and stared out the kitchen window. It was a cold windy night, and in the backyard the bare branches of the gnarled oak waved stiffly across the dark sky. It was the kind of night Holly loved. It would have been a perfect night for taking a long romantic ride with Bart in his Jeep. When she was alone with Bart, she never worried about other girls.

"It's hard dating a guy who might be voted Mr. Maryland any day now." Holly forced a laugh.

"Oh, Holly," Diana said softly, putting a hand on Holly's shoulder. "He can't help being that good-looking. It's one of the reasons you like him, isn't it?" she asked.

Holly turned around quickly and Diana's hand fell from her shoulder. "I guess," she said slowly,

15

recalling how she had just felt in the living room looking at Bart. She couldn't deny that she liked him for all the same reasons everyone else did. He was handsome, friendly, and thoughtful. But still, couldn't he concentrate on their relationship a little bit more? Did he have to be so overly friendly to everyone?

Holly sat down on a stool and propped her elbows on the counter. Sometimes she wished her best friend wasn't her boyfriend's sister. "But, Di, I don't date Bart just because he's cute and popular. You know that. I'd love him even if he didn't win these dumb pep-club contests." She toyed with her bracelet before she concluded, "But I can't help getting upset every time people start teasing him about exactly how many girls he could have if he didn't have me. It makes me feel weird — as if I'm keeping him from having the time of his life."

"Bart doesn't feel like that, and you know it," Diana said. "He's crazy about you. He's never been in love before and he's fallen hard. You're the lucky girl, Holly Daniels."

"Well, if he loves me so much, why does he flirt with those dumb girls?" Holly countered.

"Old habits die hard," Diana answered. "He's always been this way. You should have seen him in Montana — he's pretty tame these days." She suddenly gave a self-disgusted shake of her head. "Listen to me: I sound like I'm defending him. He's got his problems in the girl department." Diana sat down across from Holly and said seriously, "But he's faithful to you, you know that. He hasn't thought of dating anyone else since he met you. To him, flirting's just a game — it never leads anywhere. Holly, he really loves you. I know he does."

Hearing Diana say that didn't make Holly feel any better. Earlier tonight, she had felt terrific — so lucky, so happy. But Bart's reaction to Ted's teasing had really gotten to her. How could she expect Bart's own sister to understand? Suddenly, Holly realized she and Diana weren't alone. She looked up and breathed a sigh of relief. It wasn't Bart at the door. It was Fiona. From the embarrassed look on her face, Holly could tell she had overheard Diana's defense of her brother.

"Am I interrupting something?" Fiona poked her head further into the kitchen. Her arms were full of plates and paper cups. Laughter filtered in through the half-opened door. She looked from Diana to Holly and a sympathetic expression crossed her delicate face. "Should I leave?" She hesitated in the doorway.

"Come on in," Holly invited. She went to the sink and dabbed some cold water on her face. She didn't mind Fiona overhearing about Bart. Fiona was outspoken, but very honest. Since the benefit production of *Oklahoma!* in December, Fiona had become one of Holly's closer friends. Holly reached for a paper towel and considered confiding in her.

"Di, come out, come out wherever you are! We've got to go," Jeremy called from the hall.

Diana gave Holly's arm a reassuring squeeze.

"Hey, it'll be okay. Don't worry so much, Holly. Bart really loves you," she repeated softly before leaving the kitchen.

Holly watched the kitchen door swing open and shut a few times. Finally it came to rest.

Fiona leaned gracefully against the counter and cleared her throat. "That whole Sweets to the Sweet business got pretty weird just now, didn't it? I guess sometimes Bart's reputation gets to you."

"I didn't think anyone noticed," Holly said, looking at her feet.

"Oh, Holly, I think most of us did. But guys will be guys," she tossed off, then added offhandedly, "if we let them. I felt like saying something to Ted, but I didn't want to make a big deal out of it. He didn't really mean anything by teasing Bart."

"It wasn't Ted's fault," Holly said fairly. "What upset me was Bart. He's actually proud of the fact he'd be the winner if we held a contest to see who gets the most cookies."

Fiona ran her fingers through her short blonde hair and laughed. "Well, you know Bart's a great guy, and I think you two make a smashing couple, but he *is* a flirt. I think we all know how much he loves you, but he shouldn't always act the way he does. Someday, someone should give him a dose of his own medicine. After all," Fiona suggested with a smile, "you could very well get a ton of valentines yourself. How would Bart feel then?"

Holly couldn't help but laugh at that. "Well, we'll never find out because that's not going to happen." She stood up and stretched her slender arms high above her head. "Thanks for the compliment, but I don't have the whole pep squad following me around the quad."

Fiona rolled up the sleeves of her shirt and filled the sink with water. As she squirted detergent over the plates she said, "I just wonder how Bart would feel right now, standing in your shoes."

A few minutes later, Holly slipped out of the kitchen into the darkened dining room with Fiona's words still ringing in her ears. The party was breaking up and the commotion by the coatrack was incredible. She didn't feel like joining in. She walked to the far end of the room and stood at the end of the path of light pouring in from the hall. The problem was, Bart couldn't possibly understand how it felt dating the school Don Juan. She wished with all her heart he *could* stand in her shoes for just a few minutes. Maybe then he'd learn how much "just flirting" could hurt.

She heard him come into the room.

"Where've you been?" Bart's voice sounded strained. "I've been looking all over for you."

He crossed the room and handed Holly her hat and coat. As she took them from him, her hands trembled slightly. She kept her face turned toward the window. Bart was pretty blind when it came to his own shortcomings, but he was one of the most sensitive people she'd ever met where other people's feelings were concerned. Holly never had to tell him when she was upset or worried or scared. Bart always knew, and that was why he was more than just the guy she loved. He was also a very good friend.

Down the hall, the front door opened. A gust of wind rattled the old-fashioned chandelier over the dining-room table. Bart moved a step closer. "What's wrong? You looked so happy before."

Holly caught her breath. She kept her eyes lowered, noticing for the first time the elaborately carved feet of Mrs. Preston's antique dining-room chairs.

Bart hesitantly touched Holly's shoulder. She stood very still, then leaned slightly into his hand. It felt so strong, so reassuring. She knew in her heart that no other girl in the world mattered to Bart.

Outside it was a cold February night, but inside she was suddenly as warm as a May day. Diana was right — Bart loved her. Holly willed all her jealous thoughts to the back of her mind. Bart was with her now, not with any of those other girls. Nothing else really mattered.

"Oh, Bart," she whispered. "It was nothing really. Nothing."

To prove her point, she turned around, one arm in her coat sleeve, one arm out, and silenced Bart's questions with a sweet, slow kiss.

Chapter 2

"Hello out there, Cardinals!" Peter Lacey's voice boomed out over the loudspeakers on the Kennedy High quad. "Before we continue with our two-week-long All-Time Top Fifty Love Songs countdown, we've got our special Valentine's season feature. So here's your fave and mine, Ms. Candy Hearts, with today's edition of WKND's *Heartache Hotline*. Don't forget, today at the stroke of three I'll be interviewing the mystery gal herself. Candy, what's new in the heartache department?"

"Well, Peter," a sultry voice cooed into the mike, "I've got a letter here that's a real heartbreaker:

"Dear Candy Hearts,
I'm a junior girl and I've met this really great guy. Problem is — he's just a freshman, and he's shorter than me. I slouch every time

21

he's around so he won't feel self-conscious. He asked me to the Valentine's Day Dance, but I'm scared my friends will make fun of us if we go together. What do I do about it?
                    Signed, Born Too Soon"

"Dear Born Too Soon,
  Stand tall but wear flats! And let the grapevine buzz all it wants. True love is worth it. Besides, in case you haven't noticed, a very prestigious senior girl on the Kennedy scene set a precedent this fall and is dating a gorgeous sophomore guy. If they can do it, you can, too!

                    Candy Hearts"

  "Arrrrrgh!" Senior Chris Austin groaned at Candy Hearts's not very subtle reference to her romance with sophomore Greg Montgomery. "I'm going to kill Laurie Bennington," she threatened, looking perfectly mortified.
  "Laurie Bennington? What's she got to do with Candy Hearts?" Greg asked. "We're old news by now, Ms. President. She wasn't talking about us."
  Chris and Greg were seated on the crowd's favorite bench in a sunny corner of the quad, enjoying the sudden springlike weather and their first official outdoor lunch of the new year. Ted had spread out an old wool blanket from the trunk of his MG on the grass nearby, and Phoebe and Elise Hammond were sitting beside him.
  Phoebe looked up from her tuna sandwich and said solemnly, "Greg, the problem with being a mere underclassman is that the latest

news filters down to you so very late. Didn't Laurie tell you? *She* is the mystery lady — Candy Hearts."

"Shhhh!" Ted put a warning finger to his lips and chuckled. "Remember, it's a secret, a very big secret!"

"What secret?" Chris asked, tossing her long blonde braid back over her shoulder. "She hasn't been able to keep her mouth shut about her own secret identity. She's been broadcasting for only two days and everyone knows exactly who Candy Hearts is. I wouldn't be surprised if she goes straight to the sub shop and tells everyone who Born Too Soon is." Chris didn't like the idea of being the subject of on-air gossip but she couldn't stay angry for long. She smiled and said, "Well, I guess it doesn't hurt to set a good example."

Ted looked up and caught Greg's eye. He gave him an understanding smile. Until last August Ted had dated Chris, and he knew exactly how uptight Chris could be sometimes . . . especially when something private about her relationships got around on the quad. He rather enjoyed seeing Greg tease Chris about what used to be a pretty sensitive point with Kennedy's student body president. Though as Greg said, the fact that he was a sophomore and Chris was a senior was pretty old news, and no one had ever seemed to mind in the first place.

Greg winked at Ted and playfully tugged Chris's braid. "Come on now, be fair. Born Too Soon knew better than to sign her name, and that *was* good advice Laurie gave her." He ran his

23

finger along the border of Chris's thick Icelandic wool sweater. "I gave it to you once myself — "

"And look where it got me," Chris teased, giving an affectionate pout. Her classically beautiful face softened as she pulled Greg toward her and kissed him on the lips.

Ted turned away. Seeing Chris and Greg so in love didn't usually bother him, but today he rolled over on his stomach and picked at a clump of brown grass. Ted didn't regret breaking up with Chris. He knew now they hadn't really been that well suited to each other. Right now, however, he couldn't help feeling a little left out and lonely, surrounded by so many couples. But as Peter Lacey had told him on the way to school, being lonely was his own fault. Ted knew that better than anybody. He hadn't dated anyone in almost six months now, since the end of August when Ted had fallen in love with Molly Ramirez. She lived somewhere in Northern California now, and Ted wasn't even sure he'd ever see her again. Even so, he couldn't get her out of his mind.

Ted had met Molly after a Ramblers' baseball game down in Ocean City. He hadn't really believed in love at first sight before — it had been one of those intense summer things that was supposed to fade away to a sweet memory by the time school opened . . . but it hadn't. Ted's love for Molly had lasted all winter long and was still going strong. Deep down inside, Ted refused to believe they'd never meet again.

In the short time he had known her, Molly Ramirez had changed Ted's life. He couldn't explain exactly how. He only knew that before Molly he had looked at things one way, and now he looked at everything differently. Loving the vivacious, high-spirited California girl had somehow opened Ted's eyes. He felt life was more of an open-ended adventure.

He wasn't just Ted Mason, star quarterback, nice guy, and jock destined for a pro-football career. He was something else, besides. Meeting Molly had somehow expanded his world. He loved sports and wanted to do something physical, active with his life, otherwise he'd go crazy. Lately he'd even been thinking of a career as a diver with a marine biology research team or becoming an underwater explorer. He was strong, brawny, and loved the ocean and the feel of the sun on his back. Maybe he wouldn't be a football player at all after this year. He didn't have to go through his life being Ted Mason, jock. Before Molly, Ted never would have thought of that.

Since meeting Molly, he had learned new things about other people, too. He looked over at Greg again. A year ago, Ted would have dismissed Greg Montgomery as an okay guy who played it safe. Just sixteen years old and already geared for climbing the corporate ladder. That's how Greg looked, and in part that's what Greg was, but he was more than that, too. He had a fun, unpredictable streak. Looking at Greg, you never would have known he intended to make a fortune growing vegetables in some kind of space station circling the earth. And now Ted saw Woody as more than just a funny guy — he also had his serious, sensitive moments. His opinion of Laurie Bennington had changed, too. Ted was definitely more willing to give people a chance now than he'd been in the past, and all of his friends seemed more interesting and alive than they used to. Nothing, no one, fit in their pigeonholes anymore, and Ted liked that.

But it was already February, and his short time with Molly seemed like a very long time ago. Ted propped his chin on his hands and stared across the quad. This morning, Peter had tried to fix him up with his cousin Carol Lacey in time for the big WKND Valentine's Day Dance. Ted had almost said no, like he had said ten times before, but something stopped him this morning. Six months was a long time to wait for someone who was not going to come back.

He looked past the old chapel that served as Kennedy's theater. A dark-haired girl was jogging along the path heading toward the gym. She was wearing red shorts and white tights, and she had a great pair of legs. His heart stopped. Something about her was so like Molly, the energetic way she ran, the way she threw her head back and opened her arms to a sudden gust of wind. Ted sat up straight to get a better look. Then he shook his head and rubbed his hands across his eyes. Molly didn't have a ponytail. Molly lived in California.

"Ted," Phoebe's soft voice came from over his shoulder. "You okay?"

Ted looked up, confused. Phoebe was rebraiding her thick red hair and had moved closer to him on the grass.

26

Elise and Greg had gotten up and were playing Frisbee on the muddy ground. Elise's boyfriend, Ben Forrest, had joined them. Chris had her long legs stretched out straight on the bench and was crunching on an apple as she studied for an afternoon history quiz.

Ted reached out and gave Phoebe's braid a playful whack. Through thick and thin this year, Phoebe had been a true friend. She was the only person he'd ever told about his romance with Molly. Phoebe was the one friend he had who he knew would really understand how he felt, what he was going through, loving someone so much, knowing there was a chance they'd never meet again. Phoebe had been through something similar the year before, when she had had a long-distance romance with an actor named Griffin Neill. It was over now, and finally Phoebe was very happy with her boyfriend, Michael Rifkin. But still, Ted knew she'd understand the feeling that nothing would ever be as magical for him as falling in love with Molly at the beach last summer.

He pushed the image of Molly out of his mind and said, "I'm okay." He stared back across the quad. The dark-haired girl was gone. He poked at the soft ground with a stick and cleared his throat.

"Peter wants to fix me up with his cousin for the dance."

Phoebe leaned forward attentively. "She's very nice. I met her once at Michael's house," she said.

"I think I might take her," Ted said.

Imagining he saw Molly at Kennedy High was going a bit too far. He stood up and gave a healthy stretch. The warm sun felt good — spring was just around the corner. Ted raked his hands through his curly hair. Everything was coming to life again, and he owed that to Molly. She wouldn't like to think of him moping over her. He looked down at Phoebe and smiled. "It's about time I got back into action, don't you think?"

Phoebe scrambled to her feet and dusted off her old pink overalls. "It can't hurt," she said with a warm smile. "It's been a long time, Ted."

Holly hurried out of chem lab, stopping only long enough to scoop up some snow from a lingering patch beside the science building stairs. She was due to meet Bart at a bench by the tennis courts for a second-shift lunch. Pelting Bart with the last snowball of the season appealed to her today. She planned to tell him it was his trophy for winning the "Most Popular Guy" contest sponsored by the pep squad.

Last night, after Jonathan's party, she had had trouble going to sleep. Fiona's advice about giving Bart a dose of his own medicine somehow stuck with her. Fiona had been joking, Holly knew, but she couldn't help but wonder if making Bart jealous was the only way to get through to him, to make him see exactly how bad she felt whenever he flashed that smile at another girl. Not that Holly had the slightest idea how to go about making Bart jealous. By nature she wasn't flirtatious, and had never been very good at playing games with guys.

She preferred to walk cold into a situation and let herself be inspired. The patch of snow had inspired her just now. She laughed a low, mischievous laugh. Maybe she didn't need to flirt with anyone to get her point across to Bart. She'd just throw a bit of cold water — very cold water — in his face. Savoring that thought, she tucked the snowball in her jacket pocket and prayed that it wouldn't melt in the warm spring-like air before she reached the courts.

She was about to sit down on a bench beside a low-slung willow tree when she spotted Bart loping across the muddy grass. He was wearing sweats and his dark hair was plastered down on his head, still wet from his after-gym shower. She grinned and lifted her arm to wave. Before Bart saw her, he stopped. A vivacious redhead Holly recognized from the pep squad trotted up to him and started talking. Holly held her breath, waiting to see Bart's reaction. He looked the girl up and down and gave her a slow, warm smile. Holly's arm fell listlessly to her side. The jealousy and hurt she felt the night before rushed back full force. From where she stood, she could only imagine the look in Bart's eyes as he continued to talk easily to the girl. Holly reached into her pocket. She had a very strong impulse to hurl the snowball at the girl but she knew she couldn't throw that far. And she was really angrier at Bart than at the girl. So she just stood there, feeling very dumb and helpless, and watched until Bart finally turned and headed in Holly's direction. As soon as he spotted her, he gave her a cheerful wave and broke into an easy run.

As he reached her side, Holly dropped the snowball onto the ground. She didn't feel like teasing Bart now; she didn't even feel like eating lunch with him.

"Isn't it a beautiful day?" Bart said, throwing his arms open wide and looking from Holly to the cloudless sky and back to her again.

Holly knew he expected her to rush into his arms, to hug him as she usually did. Instead, she took a couple of steps sideways to move away from him. Apparently Bart didn't notice, because he took a deep breath and bobbed down to touch his toes. Then he flopped down on the bench and looked up at the clear blue sky. She leaned back against the tree. "I guess it is," she finally answered, toying with the droopy willow branches. They were still all brown without a trace of early spring green.

Bart sat up and unzipped his knapsack. He pulled out a takeout bag from the sub shop. "Marc picked this up when he drove Dee and Sasha over to the print shop last period. Want some?" He offered half of his Super Salami Sinker sub to Holly, and patted the empty spot on the bench beside him.

"I thought we were having lunch *together*," he said, looking closely at Holly now when she shook her head.

She dug the heel of her boot into the dirt, then studied the toe. The rich brown leather was getting all scuffed up. "Something came up, Bart," she said, finally meeting his eyes. He looked a little concerned and confused and absolutely innocent. Holly folded her arms across her chest and bit her bottom lip. "Bart — " she started, then changed her mind.

She was too upset right now to talk to him, and being this upset surprised her. She'd probably start a dumb argument, and she didn't feel like making a scene right here in the middle of lunch period. Bart obviously had no idea that the way he had just behaved had hurt her. So Holly merely said, "I crashed after the party last night, and I've got a test this afternoon. I'd better get over to the library. I've got some studying to do." She pushed her bookbag up on her shoulder and tried to sound casual. "I just came over here to tell you I can't have lunch."

Bart's face fell. He grabbed her hand as she started past the bench. Holly's body tensed up, but she didn't pull away. "Too bad," he said. "But I'll see you later. We'll meet at the flagpole at three?"

"Uh, sure," Holly stammered. She had forgotten about promising Bart a ride home on her way to the clinic.

Bart stood up and pulled Holly toward him. He pressed her close, his hands locking against the small of her back. As he bent to kiss her, Holly tried to turn away. But she couldn't. Bart's kiss was too sweet, too tender. For a fleeting moment she was tempted to forget all about the scene she had just witnessed. Like Diana had said, being a flirt was just Bart's way: It meant nothing. The way he was kissing her now meant a lot. But Holly forced herself to cut the kiss short. She had to figure out a way to tell Bart how much his flirting bothered her. Otherwise, every time it happened she would feel this badly. "I've got to go, Bart," she murmured, and started down the path. He didn't let go of her fingers until she was an arm's length off.

In the library, Holly headed for the privacy of the fiction stacks and settled down in the first available carrel. She had no intention of studying, but she felt uncomfortable lying to Bart, so she unpacked her notebook, lined up three very sharp pencils, and opened her German text.

She leaned her head back against the white-washed concrete wall and tried to sort out her feelings. What exactly was the matter with her, anyway? Why was Bart's flirting getting to her now? She knew his reputation even before she met him. It had bothered her at first and almost kept them apart. But finally Holly had trusted her heart, and she'd never been happier than she had in these past four months. Neither had Bart. Only yesterday he had told her that. But last night at Jonathan's something had snapped in Holly. Hearing about Bart winning that crazy popularity contest had made her see red. She suddenly felt like such a fool for putting up with Bart's flirting ways. None of the other boys acted that way, and plenty of them were good-looking enough to get a lot of attention. Maybe this really was Bart's way of telling her he was getting tired of her. How could she go on believing his flirting meant nothing?

Holly put her head down on the desk and buried her face in her arms. A vein in her temple was throbbing and her head ached. Her feelings just didn't make sense. They weren't logical. But she felt jealous and scared and angry, and she couldn't keep pretending she didn't. She had to make Bart see once and for all exactly how much he was hurting her. Maybe this afternoon, before she dropped him off on the way to the clinic, she would have a heart-to-heart talk with him. Maybe this time she could get him to really listen.

From the other side of the bookshelf an unpleasant laugh jolted Holly back to the present. She sat up straight and pretended she was studying. "Did you hear that dumb Laurie Bennington go through her Candy Hearts routine today?" a voice whispered cattily.

Holly wrinkled her nose in distaste. Gloria Macmillan. She'd know that voice anywhere. She quietly started to repack her things. No point pretending to study now. She couldn't concentrate anyway, and she didn't particularly want to hear whatever the curvy, dark-haired junior was gossiping about. Holly quietly pushed back her chair.

"Gloria," a second girl whispered, "do you really know that adorable linebacker who was in the musical last semester? I heard the pep squad voted him best-looking guy on campus last week. It's the first year Peter Lacey didn't get the honors."

Holly sat down again and closed her eyes. She

didn't want to stay and listen, but she felt hypnotized.

"*Know* him? Of course I know him. I was the first girl to set eyes on him the day he and that dumb blonde sister of his got to Rose Hill."

"You were?" another voice broke in.

"Did you ever date him?" someone asked.

"Ugh!" Gloria snorted. "I could have, but who'd want a guy like that —— "

"Besides, he's already got a girl friend," one of Gloria's friends interrupted.

"Well, she can have him. If he were the last guy in the world, I wouldn't want him. Can you imagine dating a flirt like that? One of these days she's going to be sorry."

"Who?" the third voice asked.

"Holly Daniels. She's the girl he hangs out with," Gloria said offhandedly. "Oh, here it is. The book I need for American lit — *The Scarlet Letter*."

Holly held her breath until she was sure the girls were out of earshot, then she peered around the side of the shelf. Gloria and her friends were already at the checkout desk Their heads were close together and they were still whispering. Holly wondered if Gloria was still talking about her — about how dumb she was to date Bart. Holly swallowed the lump forming in her throat and forced herself to stand up. Very slowly she repacked her books; she wanted to give Gloria and her gang a chance to leave. She leaned against the cool window, looking toward the library entrance, waiting to see the trio head back out onto the quad. Holly had never felt so humiliated in her life. She had never dreamed other girls talked that way about Bart. She certainly had never known Gloria had almost gone out with him when he first got to Rose Hill. Diana had never mentioned that.

At the thought of Diana, Holly again felt like an incredible fool for listening to her and allowing herself to be convinced that all Bart's flirting meant nothing. Even though she was Holly's best friend, Diana would always stick up for Bart. They had always been close, growing up so isolated on a lonely ranch in Montana. Holly watched Gloria and her friends hurry down the library steps and across the quad. Just then the warning bell rang, but Holly stood there, looking out the window beyond the tennis court toward the bench where she had just been with Bart. Remembering Bart's kiss seemed to center her. He had held her as though he loved her. She was sure of that. Holly slipped on her jacket and took a long deep breath. She really was confused.

Suddenly Gloria Macmillan's gossip seemed so silly. She tried to remember exactly what Gloria had said as she walked out the library door. That Bart was cute, that Gloria had seen him first, and that she could have dated him if she wanted to. A small smile crept across Holly's lips. She doubted very much if *Gloria* had made the decision not to date Bart. Holly's smile grew wider. Gloria was a very untrustworthy person — everyone in the crowd knew that. She was probably jealous that Holly had won Bart's heart.

The late bell rang out over the almost deserted quad and Holly broke into a run. By the time she skidded down the hall into her German class, Frau Stolz was handing out the mimeographed weekly quiz. Holly mumbled an apology and slipped into her front row seat. She struggled out of her jacket, pulled out a pen, and stared at the list of irregular verbs in front of her. But she wasn't thinking about verbs, or how much the quiz counted toward a final grade, or anything like that. She was thinking about Bart and how much she loved him and how important it was to talk to him, *today*. Suddenly she was determined to get these bad feelings out in the open between them. She had to do it before she got into the habit of letting her imagination run wild, before she forgot how to trust him.

Chapter 3

For the first time in her life, Molly Ramirez felt like a coward.

As she headed into the locker room after Ms. Molinari's last period gym class, she tried to figure out why walking up to Ted Mason and saying hello was more difficult than riding rapids, climbing Mt. Shasta, or windsurfing off Point Lobos back home. She'd been at Kennedy High more than two weeks now, and she'd seen him three times. Today on the quad she was almost certain he had seen her. She couldn't go on avoiding him forever. Besides, avoiding Ted was the last thing she really wanted to do. Avoiding him the first two times sort of made sense. She was scared and excited and very confused about the move she and her mother had made from Sausalito, California, to Rose Hill, Maryland. When she had said good-bye to Ted last August, she had thought it was forever. She had gone back to California knowing it would be a long, long time before she loved someone that much again, even though she could count the times she'd seen Ted down at the Ocean City shore on the fingers of one hand. She had felt very brave trying to get over him. She had said lots of things to him one night on the boardwalk about love like theirs being so beautiful, about learning to move on, and living just for the moment. She had really meant what she said. But Molly had to admit living for the moment hadn't worked too well for her last fall. No matter what she did, no matter whom she dated, some part of her had always been thinking of Ted. It had seemed so crazy until now, because even in her wildest dreams she had never pictured running into Ted Mason again, certainly not winding up at the same school as he was in.

Molly grabbed the shampoo out of her locker and headed for the shower. She peeled off her sweaty gymsuit and climbed into the stall. She closed the metal door behind her and leaned against it. For a moment she let herself remember last August, those hot sunny days, those breezy nights on the beach with Ted. Molly closed her eyes. She could still picture the pale yellow sand, the bright blue water that matched Ted's eyes the afternoon she met him; she could almost taste the salty wind cutting in toward shore when she looked up and first saw him. It had been the tail end of summer; her lifeguard job was almost over. Ted had been part of a crowd looking on while she rescued a little kid. The kid survived. The crowd broke up, but Ted had stayed. She had walked to the water to wash off the sand from her face and hands. When she turned around Ted was there, with a red shirt tucked in the pocket of his swim trunks. He was staring at her. She had smiled at him. She remembered that he had looked shy and confused, and she wondered why he didn't say hello right away. He didn't seem at all like a stranger standing there, and his staring hadn't made her uncomfortable. Immediately, she had felt she wanted to get to know him.

"Ramirez, you in there?" A voice echoed across the shower room. "I still need a ride to the Fitness Center."

"Yes, I'm here," Molly shouted back. "I'll be out in a minute, Katie. I didn't forget." She hastily turned the faucet on full force wondering how long she had been standing there daydreaming about Ted, forgetting to turn on the shower.

"Katie," she shouted as an afterthought, "meet me in the parking lot, at the red Subaru with California plates. I'll be there in ten minutes."

Molly began energetically shampooing her hair. She shouldn't let herself remember Ted like that. Daydreaming about him only hurt in the end. All winter long she had tried not to let herself think of him. It hadn't worked very well, but she had tried. Since her arrival in Rose Hill, she had even stopped trying. Ted was always on her mind now. Thinking of him was driving her a little crazy. Still she didn't do anything about it. She kept avoiding him, putting off the inevitable.

I'm getting to be awfully soft, she thought, pulling on her baggy red jumpsuit. Molly had always thought of herself as hardy and tough — a throwback to her pioneer Irish great-great-grandmother. Once she made up her mind to do something, she did it. That was how she'd been until recently. Molly knew exactly what she had to do now: She had to face Ted and tell him she was back and living on the other side of town. She would tell him that she had thought about it a lot, and it would be best now if they tried to be "just friends" because Molly's mother's teaching job at Georgetown University was only temporary. There was a chance of tenure for her mom, but Molly couldn't afford to believe in chances. She couldn't bear to let herself love Ted and then leave him again in June.

She swallowed hard and grabbed her towel. Telling Ted would make her heart ache and maybe his, too. Molly was suddenly glad that she had inherited more from Grandma Sheridan than big blue eyes; a freckled, turned-up nose; and an old-fashioned name. What she needed to do now took guts, and Molly wasn't sure she had enough.

Ten minutes later she had pulled on her jumpsuit, blown-dry her hair, and was in front of the locker room mirror, trying to pull her hair into a short ponytail.

She peered critically at her reflection, then caught her breath. Looking in the mirror she spotted a tall blonde girl changing into tennis whites at the end of the row of lockers. The girl looked strangely familiar. Molly stifled a sudden gasp. Of course she was familiar! Molly hadn't been on the Kennedy scene long, but she even knew her name: It was Chris Austin, the student body president. Her picture was on the front page of last week's school paper. It was the same Chris Austin Ted used to date last summer.

Molly and Chris had never met but she had seen Chris once before, one night in August, the last time she saw Ted. Kennedy's team had just won a raft race down the Potomac, and Molly had been one of the judges. She had kissed Ted on the viewing stand right in front of everyone. It wasn't a long kiss, but enough of a kiss that people probably understood that she and Ted knew each other pretty well. Molly hadn't meant to do that, because Ted hadn't told Chris about her yet. She had seen Chris out of the corner of her eye, standing to the left of the stand clutching a sailor's cap in her hand. Chris had watched that kiss, and Molly still remembered the shocked, hurt expression on her face.

Then Molly had seen the two of them walk off the stage together and into a grove of pine trees. She had waited for Ted like she had promised, in the parking lot by his red MG. She waited until the sun had set. When the moon came over the river, Molly had gone into the pines, where she found Ted and Chris holding each other very tightly. Then Chris broke away and ran toward the river. They had only been saying good-bye. Molly had realized that, but she had been startled by how beautiful Chris was. She didn't

41

look at all like the kind of girl a guy would leave easily. And Molly couldn't imagine a girl letting go of a guy as wonderful as Ted.

Now in the locker room, a scary thought began to form in Molly's head. She hadn't expected Ted Mason to wait for her. She turned away from the mirror and pretended to be searching for something in her bag. She was studying Chris out of the corner of her eye. She looked even more beautiful now. She was braiding her long silky hair and humming a very flat version of a Phil Collins ballad. Molly thought Chris looked very much in love.

Chris tossed her brush onto the top shelf of her locker and looked at a picture taped to the inside of the door. She smiled at it dreamily, then blew it a kiss. Furtively, she looked around to see if anyone had seen her and she met Molly's eyes. The two girls stared at each other for an instant. Molly held her breath. What if Chris recognizes me? she thought. Chris had seen her on the judges' stand that day, even though Molly's hair had been shorter then, and she had been wearing sunglasses. Chris bit her lip. Her long, straight nose crinkled up as she smiled foolishly at Molly. Then she awkwardly clicked the locker shut.

Molly started breathing again and managed to return a weak version of Chris's embarrassed smile. Abruptly, she ducked behind the lockers and grabbed her knapsack. She didn't want to give Chris a chance to come over and introduce herself. Molly bolted out the side door into the bright afternoon. Her friend Katie Crawford was at the far end of the parking lot, sitting cross-legged on the hood of the car with her head thrown back, taking in the sun.

With her head spinning and heart suddenly heavy, Molly ran toward Katie. Halfway there she slowed to a fast walk. She needed a minute to gather her thoughts together. She didn't want to blurt everything out to Katie. Molly hadn't told Katie anything yet about Ted, or Ocean City, or how crazy she felt ending up at Kennedy. She wasn't sure if Katie knew Ted; she wasn't sure Katie wasn't Chris's friend.

Molly hadn't expected the handsome captain of the football team to have waited for her all winter long. She had thought of him dating, but she hadn't ever thought of him loving someone new. She hadn't pictured him with a steady girl friend when she eventually walked up or phoned, saying she was back. Molly knew her feelings didn't quite make sense. She hadn't even decided exactly how she hoped their relationship would proceed. But suddenly, Molly knew clear as day that Ted was back with Chris. It must have been Ted's picture that Chris had kissed. Picturing Ted back with Chris hurt in a way Molly hadn't expected. Chris was the girl Ted had left for *her*. But when summer had ended and Molly was gone, Ted must have eventually drifted back to the golden girl.

When Holly pulled the blue Malibu into the Amoco station, the self-serve pump was closed. She steered over to the full-service island and flicked off the ignition.

"Want a Coke?" Bart asked, hopping out and digging in his pocket for some change.

Holly shook her head. "Six dollars worth," she told the attendant, not really looking at him through her sunglasses. She leaned back in her seat and watched Bart amble over to the soda machine. Some guys she recognized from school were hanging out around the repair shop entrance. Bart got a Coke and started talking to them. She was surprised Bart knew these guys — they looked like bikers, tough types that her crowd more or less avoided. Within minutes Bart had them laughing. Laughing like that in the sunlight they didn't look tough at all, just like an ordinary group of guys hanging out. Bart, as usual, gravitated to the center of the group. He was so easy with people, so sociable. As Holly watched him, she almost changed her mind. Having a heart-to-heart with Bart before she left for the clinic seemed ridiculous. Bart looked so happy, so natural standing there talking with those guys. Bart was friendly to everybody — guys, girls, bag people on the streets in downtown D.C., everybody. Maybe she was making this flirting business into too big a thing. Maybe she should forget about it. A tender smile crossed her lips. Let Bart just be Bart, she thought. So he smiles at girls sometimes. I can live with it. I can live with it all: Gloria, the gossip in the library, the pom-pon girl on the quad, that dumb popularity contest. Suddenly it all seemed so far away, so unreal.

The loud rumbling of a motorcycle turning into the service station snapped Holly out of her dreamy state. She straightened up in her seat and peered over her sunglasses. The Yamaha pulled over to the air pump and its driver yanked off a heavy black safety helmet. A cascade of blonde hair tumbled out. The driver got off her bike and stretched. Her leather pants were snug and accented her long, lean figure. A chorus of whistles sounded from over by the vending machines. Holly wheeled around and gritted her teeth.

Bart wasn't slouching against the soda machine anymore. He was standing straight and tall, grinning in the girl's direction. Holly wondered if those other guys even *had* girl friends. When the girl turned around, she looked them over. Her eyes came to rest on Bart, and her scowl gave way to a flirtatious smile. Then she bent over and began filling her back tire with air. Holly half expected Bart to go over and help her. She was pretty sure the girl was thinking the same thing. Bart didn't budge, but Holly felt like screaming anyway. He seemed to have forgotten all about Holly. She fought an impulse to drive off and let Bart find his own ride home.

"Excuse me, ma'am, do you want your oil checked?"

Holly forced her eyes away from the vending machines and back to the attendant. She looked at him a minute as if he was crazy. He might as well have asked her if she wanted to go to the moon. "Huh?" she said.

"The oil?" he asked again.

Holly looked at him for the first time. He was good-looking in a dark, rough-edged way. Here, at least, was one guy whose attention wasn't fixed on the blonde. She started to say no. Then she was inspired, remembering Fiona's words about giving Bart a dose of his own medicine. One quick look out of the corner of her eye, and she satisfied herself: Bart was still ogling the blonde, who seemed to be taking a very long time fixing her tire. Holly slipped her glasses on top of her head, and looked straight into the guy's dark brown eyes. "The oil's okay, but could you be a sweetheart and check the wiper fluid? No one's checked it in ages." She leaned out of the car window and smiled at him invitingly. Holly almost felt like gagging. She found it hard to believe other girls naturally acted this way to impress a guy.

But it worked. The guy studied her carefully, then very slowly smiled back. Holly couldn't help but respond to his very warm smile. She heard Bart's boots slowly crunching across the pavement, but she didn't turn around. Instead she read the red-embroidered name on the attendant's blue workshirt. "Matt — is that your name?" By now she was pretty sure Bart had seen her. "I don't remember seeing you around before. Did you just move to Rose Hill?" Once she started chatting, Holly found it ridiculously easy to continue her charade.

Matt leaned his elbow on the roof of the car, looked down at Holly, and laughed. "New? No, I've lived here my whole life. This is my uncle's garage. I help him out from time to time." Saying that, he traced the pattern of the Kennedy parking permit on the windshield of the Malibu.

"I go to Kennedy, too," he volunteered. "I'm a junior. How about you?"

Holly felt a twinge of either fear or guilt. She couldn't quite tell which. Flirting with someone she might actually *see* again hadn't been her plan. Not that she had had any plan. "Me, too," she said, suddenly at a loss for words.

Just then, Bart walked up. Holly pulled down her sunglasses and pulled a ten-dollar bill out of her bag. Matt counted out her change. "Thanks," Holly said, flashing Matt one more smile. "See you around!" She waved as he headed toward the next service island.

"Sure thing!" Matt waved back, then stopped and looked from Holly to Bart, who had just climbed into the passenger seat.

From the way he slammed the door, Holly knew Bart had noticed how she had smiled at Matt. He was mad. Holly savored that feeling. Fiona *had* been right. Giving Bart a dose of his own medicine was the way to go. A simple smile at one guy, and he was green with jealousy. Holly forced herself not to look at Bart and hummed Kennedy's Fight Song as she kept her eyes focused on the road.

"Who was that?" Bart asked after a long silence.

"Oh, just a guy from school."

Holly pulled off Rose Hill Boulevard onto Main Street. The light turned red. She turned to Bart and smiled sweetly. "His name's Matt Jacobs. Do you know him? He's a junior."

Bart frowned. "He's the guy that runs the Fix-

It Club. Preston's pal." As she turned down Mountain View, Holly swallowed hard. Now she'd done it. Of all the guys in the world to flirt with, she had to pick someone who was almost in her crowd. She had never met Matt before, and his name didn't really ring a bell, but she had heard about Jonathan's friend who had been such a big help at Garfield House during the Homeless Drive. She was about to change the subject when Bart continued with it.

"So, how long have you known him?"

"I don't *know* him," Holly countered, surprised at how jealous Bart sounded. "I just met him now. . . ." She paused a long meaningful moment. "While you were over at the soda machine, hanging out with the boys," she said in an accusing tone.

"What's the matter with me hanging out with the guys?" Bart asked sharply. He downed the rest of his Coke and crunched the can in his hand.

Holly pulled up to the curb in front of the Einersons' stately house. She didn't turn down the driveway and kept the engine running. She turned to Bart. "It's not the guys, Bart," she said in a hurt voice. "It's the girl. The blonde on the motorcycle. You were just about ready to hop on the back of her bike and ride off into the sunset."

Bart looked surprised. "The blonde?" He dismissed Holly's fears with a wave of his hand. "Guys always check out girls like that, Holly. It's *normal*."

"Not when the girl they're supposed to love is ten yards away watching!" Holly exclaimed, her voice catching in her throat.

48

"Are you jealous?" Bart's eyes widened. Holly didn't answer. She stared at her hands, and twisted the turquoise and silver ring Bart had given her for Christmas. "Holly." He sounded very patient, like he was talking to a child. "We've been over this before. It doesn't *mean* anything. Really it doesn't. When guys act that way with girls they don't know, it's just — " Bart floundered. He raked his broad fingers through his hair. "It's just guys being guys." He put his hand under Holly's chin and turned her face toward him. "There's no reason for you to be jealous — ever." His voice was tender, and Holly wanted very badly to believe him.

Her shoulders tensed up, and she didn't meet his eyes as she said, "Just now you were jealous — about that guy, Matt."

Bart's hand dropped from Holly's face. "That's different. I thought you were flirting with him. He sure was flirting with you." His voice was hard again.

Holly's bottom lip started trembling. She clenched her hands and forced back the tears. "Flirting for guys is okay, but for girls it isn't? Is that what you're saying? Is it, Bart?" Her voice was rising.

"It's different, that's all I said. It means more when girls flirt. Everyone knows that." Bart folded his arms across his chest.

"No, Bart!" Holly cried. "*Everyone* doesn't know that. Flirting is flirting and it hurts. You were upset just now because I smiled at a guy. But I'm not supposed to get upset when some gorgeous blonde walks by, and you act like you've never seen a girl before! Talk about double standards."

Holly was about to reach across the passenger seat and throw open the door. Bart beat her to it. Without saying another word, he jumped out and slammed the door so hard the car rocked. Holly didn't stay long enough to watch Bart head into the house. She pulled away from the curb and cursed beneath her breath. "Guys! I just don't believe them!"

Chapter 4

Karen Davis waited until Ms. Breelander's back was turned. With a sly, barely perceptible movement, she pulled the crumpled sheet of looseleaf out from under the wide sleeve of her cardigan sweater. She didn't actually have to read the note to know what it said. Every day for a week now, Marty Leonard had sent up a note from the back row of fifth period study hall. Everyday the message was more or less the same. Today's message included a Garfield cartoon cut from the local paper. "BE MINE!" the last panel said. It showed Garfield drooling over a heart-shaped pan of lasagna. Karen groaned. Marty's crush on her was getting out of hand. Today, at least, the star basketball forward hadn't sent one of his badly rhymed sonnets telling her she was as beautiful as the moon in June.

Not that Karen minded Marty thinking she was attractive, although she never thought of herself that way. She was tall and willowy with smooth, dark skin and she knew lots of people said she was even more beautiful than her older sister Wanda, who had graduated from Kennedy last June and was now studying voice in New York. Karen had been startled recently when Janie Barstow had approached and asked her to model some of Henry Braverman's designs at a special showing at Rezato's, one of Georgetown's trendiest boutiques. Janie's request had flattered Karen, but she had politely declined. Modeling was certainly something she never dreamed of doing. That was more up her sister's alley. Karen thought of herself as the plain, sensible, and practical Davis girl: the one member of her family with no ambitions to be either an opera singer, a concert pianist, or a dancer. Unlike Wanda, soft-spoken Karen wasn't cut out for a glamorous stage career. Besides, she was tone deaf and had a tin ear. But she had an uncanny nose for news and a way with words. Karen wanted more than anything to be a broadcast journalist one day. Her current heroine, Charlene Hunter-Gualt, was an Emmy-award-winning anchorwoman on the *MacNeil-Lehrer News Hour*, and someday Karen intended to host her own national news program on network TV. She was already working hard to make her dream come true.

That's why at that very moment in study hall, she was trying to finish up her article for *The Red and the Gold*. Then she planned to review her proposal for the new WKND show Peter Lacey was planning to fill the station's expanded air time. The article was due first thing tomorrow; she had to approach Peter Lacey today after school.

Karen pushed up her red glasses and stared at the clock over the chalkboard. She cupped her chin in her hands and knit her brow in concentration. Considering she was a pretty good writer, she should be able to come up with some kind of reasonable excuse by two o'clock about why she couldn't go with Marty to Friday's basketball game against Leesburg. The problem was she had run out of reasonable excuses. Every week for a month now Marty had asked her out. Each week she had said no sweetly, politely, sincerely, trying hard not to hurt his feelings. She was no more interested in Marty than she was in modeling, but he was a nice guy. Cute, sweet, sensitive — for a jock. But she felt they had about as much in common as the sun and the moon. He was tall and skinny, and she didn't like really tall guys. She preferred a boy she could look directly in the eye. Like she had told her friend Dee Patterson once, last time she dated a basketball player she got a terminal case of neck cramp.

The bell rang and Karen groaned. She was barely out of her seat when Marty appeared at her elbow. "You look great — as usual," he said, looking down at her with a smile.

"Uh, thanks," Karen mumbled, then took a deep breath. She looked up into Marty's friendly face and improvised. "Thanks for the invitation." She pointed to her sweater pocket. Marty began to smile. Before he had a chance to get too encouraged, she barreled on. "It's — it's nice of you to ask and all — but, gee, Marty, I've got this big test on Monday, and then things at *The Red and the Gold* have been pretty crazy, too. I can't go. I'm sorry," she added, suddenly feeling really awful.

Marty looked disappointed and he stared at her for a second, not saying a thing. Then he nodded slowly. "Sure, I understand. Well — see you around." With that he turned on his heels and walked out the door.

"Oh, boy!" Karen shook her head. Something in the way he said "see you around" made her know she wouldn't. He had finally gotten her message and asked her out for the last time. She really hadn't wanted to date him. Still, as she started down the crowded hall, she wondered if she was getting too picky. She hadn't been out with anyone since last year's prom, when she double-dated with Wanda and her guy, Charlie. The boy Wanda fixed Karen up with had been even taller than Marty and had been so shy neither of them had said more than five words to each other all night.

At the stroke of three, Karen marched out of *The Red and the Gold* office and down the hall. Before turning down the corridor leading to the WKND studio, she made a detour to the girls' room. As she elbowed her way to the mirror to brush her hair, she wondered if turning down Sasha's and Dee's offer of moral support was a mistake. Back in the journalism room, Karen had almost felt strong about presenting her proposal for a campus and local news feature to the popular DJ. Confronting Peter alone had seemed like the most professional way to go about selling her idea for a show. Now she wasn't so sure. She knew Peter slightly and felt pretty comfortable with him. But he was also witty, a bit slick, a fast talker, and heavily into music. Why would he bother to think twice about airing a news show? Especially one by a girl who kept a pretty low profile around school, who was soft-spoken, and who had never addressed an audience in her whole life. Sasha Jenkins was convinced Karen's proposal was exactly what Kennedy High needed, but she was the editor of the paper, not a free-wheeling DJ.

As the bathroom emptied out, Karen freshened her lip gloss and pulled her glasses down low on her nose. She carefully brushed on some dusky gold eyeshadow that made her wide-set, deep brown eyes look enormous, and tried to pat down her widly thick shoulder-length hair. She brushed off a speck of powder from her black turtleneck and stared at her reflection one last time. She wished she looked a bit more professional and a lot less scared. She tried to force a calm expression on her high-cheekboned face. But she was so nervous, she felt as if her lips were frozen into a very unnatural smile. She took about six deep breaths, then silently wished herself good luck. A few minutes later she was standing outside the WKND studio, trying to work up the nerve to knock.

Karen swallowed hard and rapped softly on the glass-windowed door. "Come off it, Davis," she muttered to herself. "You're not going to get anywhere in life being this scared!" She knocked again, this time a loud, firm, no-nonsense knock. Then she noticed the red "On-Air" light glowing above the door frame. Her knees almost buckled. Had she blown it already? Peter was obviously broadcasting, and she had actually knocked on the door. She bit her lip, closed her eyes, and tried to decide if she should walk or run down the hall. Suddenly the studio door flew open.

"Well, hello there!" a pleasant male voice boomed into the empty corridor.

Karen's eyes snapped open. She found herself staring directly into the sparkling brown eyes of a slender, shortish black guy. He was about five foot eight — almost her height. He was cute, well dressed, and lively looking. Then she realized he also looked very familiar. "I know you, don't I?"

As soon as she said it, she felt very dumb because just at that moment she figured out who he was and where she knew him from. Brian Pierson had been in Ms. Mayerwitz's study hall with her the first semester of her sophomore year. He had been much shorter then and didn't seem half as cute, or she would have remembered him better. All she could recall was Brian constantly making airplanes out of computer printout paper, and sending them whizzing out the window onto the quad, like some nerdy junior high school kid. She remembered how every day he had walked into room 201, marched directly up to Ms. Mayerwitz's desk, and announced in his big booming voice, "Brian Pierson's here." Then he'd jam the earphones to his

Walkman over his ears while the teacher grumpily took attendance. The Brian Pierson Karen remembered was a bit of a wise guy and was always listening to some weird music. But standing here outside of WKND, Brian didn't look like such a wise guy. He looked kind of interesting . . . and *interested*. In fact, the way he was looking at Karen made her forget anything else she might have remembered about him.

His approving smile widened into a grin. "I remember you, too," he declared suddenly. "I was trying to place you. We used to have study hall together. We used to have almost the same glasses." Karen had forgotten that. She self-consciously pushed her red plastic frames up the bridge of her nose. He didn't wear glasses anymore. He probably had contacts. She winced as he continued, his brow furrowed in concentration.

"Wait." He tapped his forehead. "Don't tell me your name. I have total recall. You last name begins with D. . . . Davis. Davis comma Carol — no." He corrected himself quickly. "Davis comma Karen. Karen Davis." He repeated her name and slapped his hand against his thigh. "I don't believe this. You must be Wanda's kid sister." He laughed. "So where've you been since sophomore year? I bet Wanda's been hiding you somewhere." Again he looked at Karen in a way that made her heart jump just a little. Then he leaned back against the open door.

Karen blinked, and the world seemed to snap back into focus. She put her finger to her lips and whispered, "Ssshhh. We shouldn't be talking so loud. Peter's still on the air." She pointed up to the red light. It was still lit.

"The broadcast booth's soundproof." He dismissed Karen's fears with a wave of his hand and continued, "So how's Wanda doing? Does she ever deign to come down from New York and visit the ordinary folks back home? Is she a star yet?"

Karen shifted her books to her other hip and, wondering exactly how Brian ever got to know Wanda, replied, "Oh, she's fine. She's coming home this weekend, in fact." She let out a little sigh, wishing she and Brian had something to talk about besides Wanda. She smoothed a wrinkle out of her close-fitting skirt and thought about what to say next. She definitely wanted to keep talking to this guy.

"So what brings you to WKND?" Brian asked, breaking the silence. "It was you who knocked, wasn't it?" He shaded his eyes and peered up and down the deserted hall. No one was in sight. He grinned goofily at Karen, waiting for her answer. She laughed and admitted, "I'm the one who knocked." She hesitated only an instant. The new air time on WKND wasn't a secret and news of Peter's contest would be broadcast tomorrow. "I came to see Peter about the new show," she said.

Brian's eyebrows shot up. "That's funny. So did I."

Karen's mouth fell open. "How did you find out about it?"

"Peter told me last week. Actually Michael —

you must know him, he's one of Wanda's friends — phoned last night and told me to get a proposal in before the announcement in *The Red and the Gold* tomorrow. I'm afraid the competition is going to be tough."

Karen was worried, too, but she didn't want to admit it. What kind of show was Brian proposing? "Are you a musician, like Michael?" Karen asked, hoping the answer would be no.

"Not exactly."

Karen's face relaxed.

"I'm into new music, though," Brian explained.

Karen looked blank, so he elaborated. "You know, like Philip Glass."

Karen had never heard of Philip Glass, but obviously however new his music was, it was still music — and a music show was exactly the sort of competition Karen had dreaded. "Oh boy!" she murmured. Of all the rotten luck. She had just started thinking how much she'd like to get to know this guy but now he was the competition. At that thought, the light, airy feeling inside her turned to lead.

Peter Lacey poked his head into the hallway. "What's this," he said, "a party? How come I wasn't invited?" As he worked a kink out of his neck, he asked, "Hey, Pierson, what's up? Karen, long time no see." He smiled warmly at her. Karen's smile was a bit hesitant. Face to face with Peter, and now aware of at least some of the competition, she was beginning to lose her nerve.

Brian stuffed his hands into the pockets of his

59

pants and grinned. "We're the avant-garde contenders for your new show."

Just then, Laurie Bennington drifted out of the studio and emptied out a heart-shaped box tacked to the wall. She made no effort to hide the fact that all the letters were addressed to Candy Hearts. Her alert brown eyes went from Brian to Karen and back to Brian again. "Are you two going to do a show together?" she asked in a breathy voice.

Karen felt her cheeks get hot. "Uh, not exactly," she said, then turned to Peter. "Actually *my* proposal is for a campus news show. We just happened to run into each other here in the hall." Karen wasn't quite sure why she was trying to explain away Brian's presence.

Laurie arched her eyebrows and gave Brian an encouraging smile. "What fun!" she cooed, then turned back to Karen. "You're lucky. I'm always wanting to do a new show."

Laurie leaned back against the door frame, showing off her shapely legs and her slick red leather miniskirt. "It's sad thinking about graduating in June. This new air time would have been perfect for me. Like I just said in my interview with Peter, I would have loved to continue this Candy Hearts show next — " She caught Peter's eye, "Ooops," she giggled, then lowered her voice to an exaggerated whisper. "It's supposed to be a secret."

Karen stifled a groan, and then caught Brian's eye. He was the first to burst out laughing. Karen began to giggle a little, too. Laurie had never struck her funny before.

As soon as he recovered, Brian reminded gently, "Laurie, everyone *knows* who Candy Hearts is."

Laurie smiled sheepishly, and admitted, "Keeping secrets has never been my strong point!" She checked her heart-shaped watch and gasped, "I have to run to the library. Believe it or not, some of these letters are pretty serious. A lot of kids write with real problems, and I'm trying to answer all of them. Mr. Evans in the counseling office gave me a list of books to check out before I go home." With that, she tugged her soft leather bag up higher on her shoulder and hurried off, her high-heeled boots clicking against the linoleum floor.

Peter sank down against the wall and moaned. "Even if she hadn't told everyone who Candy Hearts is, they would have guessed. Have you ever seen anyone so good at dressing the part?"

Karen and Brian burst out laughing again. As she wiped the tears from her eyes, Karen looked sideways at Brian. She liked how it felt laughing with him. In fact, she was trying to remember when she had felt so comfortable sharing a joke with a guy before.

Peter ushered them into the cramped anteroom of the broadcast studio. Karen had never been there before and her eyes widened as she looked around the pleasantly cluttered space. Colorful promo albums and rolled-up posters littered every surface. The record library was neatly arranged on several shelves, which figured, since Peter's assistant, girl friend, and fellow DJ — Monica Ford — was a whiz at organization. Peter was the quick-moving, fast-rapping voice that made the Kennedy station a local success, but Monica was the person who held it all together.

Karen sat down in a folding chair and flipped through some of the albums. She had never seen so many records in her life. At the far end of the room, beyond the glass-windowed door, was the tiny broadcast studio itself. A couple of turntables and a microphone formed the centerpiece of the work area. A giant red clock with a prominent second hand hung over the window; a formidable array of buttons, switches, knobs, and lights nestled in the control panel against the wall.

Karen gulped. She had been so concerned with thinking out the show proposal, she had totally forgotten about the broadcasting part. Worrying about the competition had made her forget about how technical broadcasting was. Karen didn't think of herself as a person who couldn't learn technical stuff. Lately she had gotten pretty good with her friend Dee's camera. But Dee had been there to teach her. Now she was sitting inside a radio station about to sell herself and her show, without knowing the first thing about radio. She felt even more nervous when she remembered that Brian had been one of those computer, video, and technical freaks back in the tenth grade. She was sure the control panel of a space shuttle wouldn't intimidate him.

Karen looked up. Brian was straddling a wooden chair, talking animatedly with Peter. Not exacly with Peter, Karen realized, but *at* him.

He had cleared a space on the floor, had spread some tapes and records, and was handing Peter a sheaf of papers. From where she was sitting, Karen could tell the proposal had been done on the computer room printer downstairs. She nervously fingered the manila envelope in her hand. She had been holding it so tightly, the edges were all bent over. Her proposal was inside, probably wrinkled by now. It had been typed on the newspaper's old manual typewriter, the one Sasha always said inspired her.

Karen felt like kicking herself. While she had been gaping at her new surroundings like a kid on her first day of school, Brian had gotten a head start — actually, his second head start, on selling his idea. His first head start was because Brian was into music. Peter would want a music show over a news show any day. Karen half wanted to get up and edge her way out of the room — she wasn't sure she wanted to go through with this. From where she sat, she could tell Brian's smooth-talking about new music, and a show called *Soundings*, had the usually unflappable Peter Lacey spellbound.

Peter's hand suddenly flew up and he broke into Brian's presentation. "Hold it! Hold it!" He pushed his wavy brown hair off his face and said with a laugh, "Brian, hold your horses. *Soundings* sounds great to me. But I'm hoping for lots of great ideas. Most of Kennedy doesn't even know there's a contest going on, and you're rushing off down the stretch trying to beat everyone to the finish."

Karen's mouth fell open. Sasha was right.

Peter was a fair-minded person. He turned to her and smiled in apology.

"Karen hasn't even had a chance to tell me what her news show is about." He took the envelope from her hand. "Is this your proposal?"

"Yes," was all she said at first, then she mustered up her courage. Peter had just given her an opening. Maybe Brian was heading for some sort of finish line before the race even started, but she could at least let Peter know she was serious about being at the starting gate. "Kennedy is a big school, with a lot going on. The paper comes out once a week, and it can cover some of the news in depth. But every day kids are doing things, making news: sports news, academic news. How many people do you think even know we have a debating team at Kennedy, let alone realize it's the top-ranked team in the state?" She looked from Brian to Peter and felt faintly surprised that they actually looked interested.

"I didn't," Brian said solemnly.

"That's why we need a news show," she declared triumphantly. As she talked about her plans for *What's News* her serene face grew animated and her eyes sparkled. When she stopped to catch her breath, Peter startled her by jumping up and applauding, his green eyes glowing with approval.

Just as she started to tell him about the tie-in with local Rose Hill news he shouted, "Whoa!" He took her proposal and the larger envelope Brian had restuffed with his tapes and other paraphernalia and said in an encouraging tone, "You could have sold me! But like I told Pierson here, I'm not buying yet."

"But you like it!" Karen cried, unable to contain herself.

Peter wagged a warning finger in her face. "Yes. But I like lots of things. *Soundings* appeals to me, too," he added fairly.

Karen tried not to look too disappointed. For a minute, she had actually believed she had sold her show — lock, stock, and barrel — to Peter. Now she wasn't sure. Especially when Peter turned to Brian and said, "Did you hear WRRK is having a Midnight Dieter Music Marathon next week?"

"Yeah. I was thinking of taping it."

"Why don't you come over to my place? I've got a new sound system you might want to check out," Peter invited.

Karen's hopes instantly withered. She suddenly felt crazy letting herself believe even for a minute that Peter would choose *What's News* over *Soundings*. And like he said, he hadn't even gotten any other entries yet for his informal contest.

"Anyone game for the sub shop?" Brian asked, looking in Karen's direction.

"Do you have to ask?" Peter dropped in a mock faint onto his creaky swivel chair. He grabbed his leather bomber jacket and held open the studio door for Karen.

Karen walked into the hall and glanced up, surprised to find Brian standing so close to her, looking straight into her eyes. As she rearranged her bag on her shoulder, the nubby fabric of his jacket sleeve brushed her hand. Her heart skipped a beat. Then she edged away and shook her head. "No, I've got to get home," she lied, starting the opposite way down the hall. She didn't have to get home, but she certainly didn't have to subject herself to listening to Brian and Peter talk about music. It was too depressing. Under any other circumstances she would have loved to go somewhere with Brian and get to know him. But Brian wasn't just a guy, he was competition — and getting to know him the way she wanted felt wrong. She wasn't ready for this yet.

Chapter
5

Phoebe Hall struggled to keep a straight face as she made her way through the heavy rush-hour traffic heading into Georgetown. Her eleven-year-old brother Shawn was beside her on the front seat of the family station wagon explaining he had finally fallen in love. The lucky girl was none other than his new akido teacher. Between sighs, he filled Phoebe in on her vital statistics. "She's from California. And she's so pretty. And she's a black belt."

"A bit old for you, no?" Phoebe interjected, casting a glance in her brother's direction. His freckled face was beaming and he was wearing the Mr. Spock ears that belonged to his best friend, Paul. He had won the right to wear them for a week in a *Star Trek* trivia contest.

"Doesn't matter. I'll grow up some day. I don't intend to marry her until I'm old enough. I'm not that much shorter than her now," Shawn explained cheerfully. He propped his feet on the dashboard and looked out of the corner of his eye at his sister. Phoebe pretended not to notice. Their mother never let Shawn put his dirty sneakers on the dashboard.

"Well, I don't think you should wait that long," Phoebe suggested, a wicked gleam lighting up her big green eyes.

"Huh?" Shawn gulped. "You mean I should ask her to marry me now?"

Phoebe stifled a laugh. "No," she said, forcing a serious tone. "But you could send her a valentine. It *is* almost Valentine's Day."

Shawn shoved his Baltimore Orioles cap back on his curly red hair and gave a low, appreciative whistle. "Why didn't I think of that? Chocolates, perfume, flowers? Uh, Phoebe, what do you suggest? I knew I shouldn't have raided my piggy bank last week. Seeing *Rocky* for the fourth time was definitely not worth it." He groaned and out of his pocket pulled a limp dollar bill that looked like it had been through the wash a couple of times.

"A Sweets to the Sweet personalized Valentine's Day cookie is what I'd recommend. I think Kim has special rates for people under fourteen," Phoebe replied. "I told you about Kim's new cookie business."

"Oh, wow!" Shawn's face opened into a wide, toothy smile. "What a great idea! Kim bakes the best cookies in the whole world."

"I'll order a cookie for you this week. What's her name?"

"Miss Ramirez," Shawn said and settled into his seat with a contented squirm.

Phoebe cleared her throat as she pulled into a parking space in front of the Georgetown Martial Arts, Fitness, and Dance Center. "You have to find out her first name. You can't send a cookie to a girl you intend to marry without knowing her first name."

Phoebe followed Shawn upstairs and into the studio. Some other children were already warming up in the corner. She stopped in her tracks when she saw the teacher. She had expected someone closer to her mother's age, or at least in her twenties. The teacher looked about Phoebe's age. She was more cute than pretty, with curly dark hair and a pert, upturned nose. Her soft white pants and baggy shirt contrasted strongly with her dramatic coloring and dark tan. She looked too small to be very strong, but Phoebe noted the black belt she wore at her waist. Phoebe liked her instantly and had the eeriest but she knew black belts were pretty advanced. The teacher walked up to Phoebe with her hand outstretched and a broad smile on her face. Phoebe liked her instantly and had the eeriest feeling she'd seen her somewhere before.

"Hi," the teacher said. "We have a class for teenagers later this evening."

Phoebe held up her hands in protest and laughed. "I'm not sure I'm about to try akido just yet. I'm just dropping off my brother, Shawn. I'll pick him up later."

Ten minutes later Phoebe walked into the Albatross bookstore and remembered she forgot to ask Shawn's teacher her first name.

"Hi, Pheeb!" Sasha called out. Phoebe looked around the cozy, well-stocked store, then grinned as her friend's head popped up from behind the counter. "Did you deposit the little scoundrel at the fitness center?" Sasha asked, pushing her long dark hair off her face.

"Freedom for an hour!" Phoebe sighed. Her parents were in Boston at a Legal Aid convention and Phoebe had been left in charge of the house and Shawn. "There must be an easier way to earn a living," she moaned, and collapsed in one of the easy chairs in front of a wall of wooden shelves. One of the nicest things about the Albatross was that Sasha's parents believed people should come and read books, not just buy them. They never minded Sasha's friends coming into the store and just hanging out when Sasha worked after school.

Phoebe propped her feet up on a table and randomly thumbed through a glossy paperback romance lying nearby. The heroine on the cover was dark-haired with deep blue eyes. She reminded Phoebe of Shawn's teacher. Phoebe wondered aloud, "Ever get the feeling you've seen someone before? That you even know their name, but you know that it's impossible?"

Sasha sighed. "I've read about that kind of thing. It's terribly romantic. Sometimes people dream about people they haven't met yet. Then they meet them. Psychologists have all sorts of theories about it, but I think it's magic."

Phoebe glanced over at her friend. "Sasha,

you're such a dreamer. Sometimes I think you must still believe in the Tooth Fairy." Sasha giggled and pulled a carton of sale books across the floor. She settled at Phoebe's feet and began pricing them with a felt-tipped pen.

Phoebe looked once more at the back cover, then put the book back on the shelf. She began twiddling a strand of her long red hair, and her pretty, expressive face was screwed up in thought. "Still, I met Shawn's teacher just now, and I can't shake the feeling I've seen her before. I know her from somewhere. I just know I do." She pounded the arm of the chair.

"You won't remember that way," Sasha said wisely. "It's like a word on the tip of your tongue. You've got to stop thinking about it, then all at once — presto! — it's there."

Suddenly Phoebe jumped up. She was staring down at Sasha, aghast. "I don't believe it!" she whispered, then clamped her mouth shut. She had finally made the connection. She knew where she had seen Shawn's teacher before, and if her suspicions were correct, she wasn't sure sharing them with Sasha, or any other friends, was such a good idea. In fact, mentioning that Ted's summer girl friend from California was teaching in Georgetown at a martial arts school might turn out to be a disaster.

Phoebe remembered her first name now — Molly. Molly Ramirez. But why didn't Ted know Molly was back in Maryland? He'd been pining over her since last summer, and now he didn't even know she was here. What was going on? Phoebe had an impulse to drive back to

Georgetown, confront Molly, and explain she knew Ted and all about their romance last summer. But then Phoebe's stomach knotted up. In Molly's shoes, she'd feel pretty weird if a perfect stranger walked up and said she knew so much about her. No, she was sure Molly wouldn't appreciate that. Then Phoebe remembered Sasha. If she stayed, she'd be tempted to tell her about Molly and she knew Ted was counting on her not to tell anyone. She thought quickly.

"Er — I just remembered, Sasha. I have to run a few errands before I pick up Shawn," she said hesitantly. She bolted out the door and yelled behind her, "I'll talk to you later."

Once she got outside, Phoebe slowed to a walk and wandered around the shopping center, looking in windows. She had a half hour to kill before Shawn's class was over. She dreaded seeing Molly again. Phoebe felt embarrassed and confused now that she thought she knew who the girl was and she had a crazy impulse to call Ted and tell him she had just seen Molly. Phoebe knew she really wouldn't do something like that. After a while, she got into her car and she drove around Rose Hill. She passed the sub shop. All the kids were there, she could tell from the cars: Peter's gold VW bug; Laurie's Mustang; Janie's green Plymouth; Jonathan's old Chevy, Big Pink. She didn't feel like seeing any of them so she headed for Mario's to grab a soda. When she saw Chris's blue Chevette there, she decided against going in. Chris was the last person she wanted to run into now. Chris and Ted had weathered their breakup well. They were still friends, but Phoebe's intuition told her Chris was not the person to confide in about Molly. She drove back to Georgetown and sat huddled in the car outside the fitness center, trying to figure out what to do next. Whatever it was, she wanted to be very careful not to start trouble, and above all, not to hurt Ted.

Chapter
6

Holly and Bart had never had a fight before. That was the long and short of it, and Holly was scared. The sensible part of Holly knew that one argument didn't mean a relationship was over, but she just felt overwhelmed with doubt about what was going on between them. Holly had never loved anyone as much as she did Bart, and she knew they had to figure out a way to work things out. Giving him a dose of his own medicine had backfired, but she had to figure out something else. . . . Holly still saw red every time she pictured Bart ogling that blonde on her motorcycle.

For the fourth time in ten minutes she forced herself to stop pacing up and down her small bedroom. She had paced it so many times she knew exactly how many steps it took from the edge of the bed to the old-fashioned low window-sill: eight. She had a wry thought that she was about to wear a hole in the oval hooked rug she had bought recently at a flea market. Usually Holly's room felt like a refuge — a warm, comfortable place that was all her own. With the help of Phoebe, Diana, and Brenda she had spent weekends scouring area junk stores and thrift shops to furnish it. Now old-fashioned oval frames with sepia-toned photos of turn-of-the-century strangers decorated one wall. The green glass shade on her brass desk lamp softened the light, and the dainty yellow floral wallpaper Holly had hated when they first moved into the house looked just right with the old-fashioned furnishings. But tonight her cozy room felt more like a prison.

She flopped down in her reading chair and propped her feet up on the antique patchwork quilt at the foot of the bed. She let out an exasperated sigh. Letting herself worry so much about Bart wasn't doing any good. For the umpteenth time that night she made a resolution to keep her mind on her homework and off Bart. She had a report due early next week for literature class; each kid in the class had pulled the name of a Russian novel out of Mr. Wiley's Rose Hill Softball League hat. The luck of the draw had left Holly with *Anna Karenina*. She had thought she would hate the thick book, but she had devoured the passionate love story in record time. Page by page, she ached for Anna's plight — sacrificing child, reputation, and family to be with the man she loved. She was nearly at the end now. Holly picked up the dog-eared paperback and pulled out the emboidered bookmark Sasha had given her for Christmas. With a great effort of will, she forced her eyes to stay on the page. After two paragraphs a tear started down her face. She wasn't sure if it was because of the book, or whether it was the thought of Bart, and today's scene with Matt Jacobs.

A gentle rap on her door roused her. "Honey, can I come in?" A second later Holly's mother poked her head into the room. Holly quickly wiped away the rolling tear. She didn't want to be caught crying. Her mom had been so happy lately, looking forward to her marriage to Bruce. The smile quickly faded from her mother's face. "Holly, what's wrong?" Mrs. Daniels said, crossing the room toward her.

"This book — it's so sad," Holly improvised and made a dramatic gesture as she pulled a handful of yellow tissues from the box on her desk. She blew her nose and avoided her mother's eyes.

Her mother cocked her head and looked down at the novel lying open on Holly's lap. "That's putting it mildly," she said in a relieved voice. She continued to study her daughter's face carefully. "I guess you're busy," she said. Something in her voice invited Holly to confide in her — but Holly held back. She wasn't used to talking to her mother about guys, and she wasn't sure this was the best time to start — right after her first fight with Bart.

Holly wavered a second before deciding to keep her troubles private, then suddenly noticed the soft blue dress draped over her mother's arm.

The price tag from Saks was still attached. "Oh Mom!" she cried, scrambling to her feet. "Is that it? Is that your dress for the wedding?" Holly rubbed her hands against her jeans before delicately fingering the fabric.

Her mother pushed back her straight dark hair and bit her lip. "Yes, do you like it?" She held it up against herself for inspection. "I need to shorten it. I wondered if you'd put it on so I could pin up the hem."

"You bet!" Holly said. She and her mother were about the same height and, even though Holly was slightly slimmer, they often wore each other's clothes. Holly enjoyed playing mannequin for her mother, who was a whiz with a needle and had in the past made a lot of Holly's clothes. She pulled off her sweat shirt and jeans and slipped the silky dress over her head. She turned once in front of the mirror. "It's beautiful . . . or would be without these." She pulled off her knee socks and slipped on a pair of blue heels she had worn last year to a cousin's wedding.

Her mother knelt on the floor and began marking the hem with dressmaker's chalk. After a moment's silence she asked, not looking up, "Is something wrong between you and Bart?"

Holly closed her eyes and let out a quiet sigh. As usual, her mother had read her mood perfectly. After a moment's hesitation, Holly said softly, "Yes, I guess so."

"Do you want to talk about it?"

"I don't know. It's just—" She faltered.

"He's so good-looking, Mom. All the girls notice him . . . and sometimes I get upset." Her voice shook slightly.

Holly's mother sat back on her heels and looked up. "So, you're a little jealous. I can understand that," she said sympathetically.

Holly folded and unfolded her hands and shrugged. "Yes." She was afraid to say too much. She wondered what her mother would think if she told her what had happened with Matt at the gas station.

"Well, have you talked to Bart about it?" Mrs. Daniels asked. "Whatever's going on between you, being direct and open about it is the best policy. Letting things fester inside just makes matters worse. And having the blues and moping — and reading sad novels" — she gestured toward the book on Holly's bed — "doesn't help at all. You'll only make whatever's going on worse. More trouble comes from misunderstandings and lack of communication than anything else."

Holly nodded thoughtfully as her mother slipped out of the bedroom. The advice rang true. Holly took off the dress, yanked on her jeans, and as soon as she heard the sound of her mother's bathwater, Holly reached for the phone. She would call Bart. Her hands were a bit clammy and her heart was pounding as she started to dial. But awkward as it might feel, talk-to him would certainly help clear the air. She didn't like the idea of going to sleep feeling this hurt and angry and confused inside. She probably wouldn't even be able to sleep. Holly still loved Bart, and suddenly the most important thing in the world seemed to be to tell him that.

Before she finished dialing, the doorbell rang. "Holly, I'm in the tub, can you get it?" her mother called from down the hall.

Holly hung up the phone and heaved a sigh. Whoever was at the door, she'd get rid of them fast and come back up and call Bart before she lost her nerve. She hurried down the stairs and threw open the door.

She gasped. "Bart!" Her whole face lit up.

"Whew, I was hoping you'd be here," he said with a nervous smile. His big frame filled the narrow doorway and he stood there a moment, shifting from foot to foot. Holly thought how odd it was; Bart seldom looked awkward. "These are for you," he said, abruptly shoving a bunch of carnations into her hand. She took them and searched Bart's eyes. He looked so worried, so concerned. He still loved her, too.

Holly smiled shyly and said, "Thanks for the flowers." She looked at the floor and tried to keep from laughing.

"You aren't going to believe this," she said, curling her bare toes on the welcome mat and wishing she was wearing something other than her torn Camp Chesapeake sweat shirt and paint-stained jeans. "I was just trying to call you."

Bart's smile widened. He leaned his long muscular body against the door frame and shoved back his cowboy hat. He looked almost relaxed again. "Uh — can I come in? Or am I interrupting something?" he said casually, looking past Holly's shoulder as if expecting to find someone else in the living room.

Holly noticed him looking behind her. For a second, she didn't realize what he was looking for. Then she understood. Matt. She exhaled sharply and said, "Like I said, all you were interrupting is a phone call to you. Come on in." Holly ushered him through the door. "Mom's in the tub. I'll go upstairs and tell her you're here."

She detoured through the kitchen and put the carnations in an empty bottle. She filled it with water, then set it on the counter and buried her nose in the flowers. They had a sweet delicate scent. Bart had never brought her flowers before, but somehow it was like him. He was as scared of losing her as she was of losing him. They were going to be able to work this trouble out.

When Holly came down again, she was wearing her aqua cashmere sweater and had tied a filmy matching scarf through her hair. Upstairs she had resolved to talk things out with Bart, to explain her feelings. He was leaning back on the cushion-strewn sofa, staring out the window. The drapes weren't drawn. The warm afternoon thaw had ended and long icicles dangled from the roof, glistening in the light cast from the street lamps.

"I'm glad you're not leaving this house when your mom gets married next month. I like it here — it's so comfortable, so homey," Bart said.

Holly nodded, then cleared her throat. Bart seldom made small talk, only when he was nervous. Part of her wanted to rush over to the couch and throw her arms around him and tell him whatever was wrong between them didn't matter. They should just forget the whole scene at the gas station today. What mattered was how much she loved him, how much he loved her. She hesitated a moment, then sat on the edge of the rocking chair opposite Bart. She folded her hands in her lap.

"I'm sorry for what happened today." Her voice sounded absurdly loud in the quiet room.

Bart leaned forward, his elbows on his knees. "Oh, Holly," he said. "Me, too. I didn't realize I could feel so jealous," he admitted.

Some of the tension went out of Holly's shoulders.

"It's never come up before, really," Bart continued, looking awkwardly down at his cowboy boots. "I guess until you think you might lose someone, you don't really know — "

"Oh, Bart," Holly interrupted. "You're not losing me because I talked to some guy in a gas station. I told you he meant nothing. I never even saw him before. The point is, you out-and-out flirt with almost every girl you see, and it upsets me. Then you tell me it never means a thing. So if I flirt, or if someone flirts with me, why are you so sure you're going to lose me? I just don't get it," she said. "Don't you see, Bart, it makes me nervous sometimes to see the way you act with other girls. It makes me feel like I don't mean anything to you."

"But Holly, when I talk to girls I'm just being friendly," Bart protested, then instantly looked repentant. "I don't mean that the way it sounds. Besides," he added after a pause, "the point is, I love you, Holly. I'm scared of losing you." With that, Bart was on his feet and by her side. He reached his hands out toward her. She didn't hesitate an instant. She allowed him to draw her close. Behind them, the rocking chair squeakily rocked a few seconds before slowing to a halt.

"I'm scared, too," Holly whispered into his sweat shirt. The sweet outdoorsy scent of him drove away every protest, every argument in Holly's head. She pressed herself against his chest and squeezed her eyes shut. If only it could always be this way, just her and Bart. No pep squad, no fans, no one teasing him about being a real Don Juan.

When they were alone like this, no other girl existed for Bart. Holly knew that. But back at school, in the halls, strolling around the quad, around the Rose Hill hangouts, Bart was all eyes for any girl who had eyes for him. Holly pulled back from his loving hold and looked up at him, her large hazel eyes clouded with tears. Before she could say a word, Bart tilted her chin up toward his face and very gently kissed her. The floor seemed to reel beneath Holly's feet, and somehow she found herself on the couch with him, staring deep into the blue pools of his eyes.

"So, tell me," Bart said after a long silence, "at the end of tonight's episode of *True Love Stories*, are the most beautiful girl from Kennedy High and the cowboy from Montana still friends?" The old flirtatious twinkle was back in his eyes.

Holly couldn't help but grin. A few weeks ago on a double date with Diana and Jeremy, they had invented a game called *Soaps*, thinking up outrageous ongoing plots for nighttime TV serials with cliff-hanger endings. "At *least* that, but you have to tune in next week."

"And find out the true identity of the mystery man at the gas station?" Bart said glibly, but his laugh sounded forced and his eyes narrowed slightly. Holly's shoulder tightened. Just then she heard her mother's footsteps padding down the upstairs hall. She and Bart sprang apart on the couch, and Holly smoothed her sweater back over her jeans. Bart tenderly reached over and clumsily began retying the scarf in Holly's hair. The filmy material had slipped down around her neck.

Holly drew back slightly, not enough for Bart to really notice. She took the scarf from his hands and tied it herself. She kept her face turned away from him and tried to sort out her thoughts. His kisses proved he loved her. She'd be a fool to believe otherwise. Yet she felt strangely let down. Sure, they had just made up, but nothing had changed. Bart still thought he could go on flirting — he just didn't understand. And he was still nervous about Matt. Holly got up, and Bart stood behind her, his hands on her shoulders. She didn't turn to give him a goodnight kiss. She was trying to digest the fact that Bart expected her to trust him no matter how many girls threw themselves at him or how much he flirted back. That was just something he did, like breathing. But the bottom line was, just her talking to a guy made him jealous. So jealous that after all the explanations, he still didn't trust her.

"See you tomorrow," he said softly, drawing her alongside him as he headed for the door.

Holly nodded, then finally trusted herself to meet his eyes. She ran her finger down the side of Bart's strong square jaw. His skin was rough from having spent so much of his life outside on the wide Montana plains. "I love you, Bart," she said softly, then lifted her face toward him for a gentle good-night kiss.

As she closed the door behind him, her thoughts were whirling. She had taken her mother's advice and had talked to him as openly as she could. It still hadn't worked. Holly was sure Bart loved her, but she had to make him see that his flirtatious ways had to stop. Being a guy was no excuse for his actions. She wondered who she could ask for help. Diana was her best friend, but Diana had already told her a million times that Bart wasn't going to change and that he didn't mean anything by acting the way he did. Besides, she needed advice from someone more objective than Bart's sister. Someone who didn't know either Holly or Bart.

Holly wandered into the kitchen and poured herself a glass of milk. She sat at the counter staring blankly at the milk carton. The forlorn face of a missing child stared back at her, but she hardly noticed. Holly cocked her head as if listening to something. A slow smile crept across her face. "I've got it!' she said, and jumped up. She put her glass in the sink, grabbed the bottle full of flowers, flicked out the downstairs lights, and bounded upstairs two at a time.

" 'Night, Mom!" she cried as she bolted into her room and sat down at her desk. As Holly began to write, she wondered if all complicated questions had such simple solutions.

Chapter
7

Jeremy Stone peered through the viewfinder of his camcorder and motioned for Brian to begin his demonstration. The computer room was uncomfortably hot with lights, and as Brian flicked on the synthesizer console he wondered nervously if the heat was going to make the system crash. He and Jeremy had been videotaping for over an hour now. Instead of beginning his rap about programming music on the computer, he tugged his close-cropped black hair and frowned up into the camera.

"I think we should take a break."

Jeremy raised his blue-gray eyes to the ceiling and groaned. He turned off the camera and tapped his foot impatiently. "Brian, what's with you? An hour's work and I don't have more than two minutes of usable footage."

Brian made an apologetic face. "Sorry about that, but these lights are really hot. Bad for the equipment." He flicked out the floods and pulled a can of soda out of his knapsack. It was still slightly cold. He took a sip and passed the can to Jeremy, then hoisted himself up on top of the Formica table running the length of one wall.

"So how's the radio show coming along?" Jeremy asked, pulling up a typing chair and sitting down.

Brian sat up a little straighter. Jeremy had just given him the opening he'd been looking for. Since yesterday afternoon he had been thinking about Karen. Though he had forgotten her name at first, he remembered her face very well from Mayerwitz's study hall. He had tried hard to get her attention back then, but she hadn't seemed at all impressed with his paper airplane routine. Since sophomore year he hadn't really seen her around. Brian wondered who she hung out with, exactly what she did for *The Red and the Gold*, and if she had a boyfriend. He was afraid of getting his hopes up. Yesterday, he had gotten the feeling that she was as interested in him as he was in her. Today, he was wondering if he had imagined the whole thing. Brian wanted to believe she was interested, but she had left so abruptly and hadn't wanted to go to the sub shop where they could have spent some time getting to know each other. He knew he wanted to see her again, but he wasn't quite sure how to arrange it.

Brian liked to give the impression he was a cool, laid-back guy who had a way with girls, but he actually hated asking girls out on dates. He feigned disdain for the dating game. If you liked someone and they liked you, things just happened naturally. At least, that's what he told his friends. The truth was he was afraid girls — especially beautiful, sophisticated girls like Karen — wouldn't give him the time of day if he asked them out. Calling a girl cold and asking her out scared him out of his wits. It would have been so much easier if Karen had gone with him and Peter yesterday to the sub shop. Then he could have offered her a ride home. She might have said no, but it would have been an opening.

"The show," he said, shrugging nonchalantly. "Peter said he wants all the proposals in before he really considers them. But a funny thing happened. At the studio yesterday I ran into — " Brian stopped himself. He had almost said an old friend. He didn't know how well Jeremy knew Karen, if at all, but he'd beter not take a chance. "A girl I know — Karen Davis. Know her?"

"Hmmm." Jeremy gulped down another mouthful of soda. "She's friends with my sister. Fiona, Dee, and Karen hang out a lot together." Jeremy spun around on the chair, dragging the toe of his loafer across the linoleum. He stopped long enough to grab the camcorder. As he spoke with Brian, he intently began taping the motion of his own foot.

"Really?" Brian was surprised. Karen sounded like part of Jeremy's crowd, but he didn't remember ever seeing her at the sub shop. "I guess she's pretty busy with the paper," Brian said. He cracked the knuckles of his slender hands.

"And honor society. I get the impression she

studies a lot." Jeremy stopped spinning in his chair and looked intently at Brian. "Why are you so interested? Or should I ask?"

"She's the competition," Brian responded instantly, although he hadn't thought of her like that before. "She's proposing a news show. She gave a pretty impressive rap about it to Peter. I wanted to know what I'm up against." He stood up and stretched. "She sounds formidable."

Jeremy cleared his throat. "Yeah, she's pretty smart, and she's a good reporter. She's also rather pretty," he said, eyeing Brian closely to see his reaction.

"I can't say I didn't notice that," Brian said. He leaned back casually against the table and flashed Jeremy what he hoped was a very knowing smile.

"You're a sly one!" Jeremy swatted Brian with the strap of his camera. "So why don't you ask her out? She's not dating anyone I know of."

Brian didn't answer. Not out loud. But of course that's exactly what he intended to do now that he knew she wasn't going out with anyone. He'd head for the sub shop after school and try to track her down. Charlie Walker was playing at Toons Saturday night. Brian had heard Wanda was going with Michael and Phoebe, and Peter had mentioned he might turn up with Monica. Maybe Karen would go with him.

Brian deliberately flicked the floods back on. "Ready for work?"

"The question is — are you?" Jeremy quipped, and set his camera rolling.

* * *

Whistling the upbeat refrain to "Singing in the Rain," Bart walked into the cafeteria and practically choked. The air was thick and stale and the noise was deafening. The song died on his lips and his eyes strayed toward the floor-to-ceiling windows lining the west wall. Outside, an icy drizzle fell and fog blanketed the quad. It looked so unreal, so deserted, like the secluded meadow beyond the upper pasture back home.

Bart shook off the memory of Montana and tried to focus on the here and now: rainy day fourth-period lunch at Kennedy. As much as he missed his old life on the family ranch, he loved his new life here. In a few minutes he'd be in the middle of his crowd of friends — joking, laughing, and thoroughly enjoying himself. And Holly would be with him. Last night they had made a date to meet for lunch. Thinking of last night, Bart felt a funny shiver go down his spine. He couldn't quite shake the feeling that yesterday he had almost lost Holly, and he wasn't sure why. But it didn't matter. It had been such a silly argument and they had made up. He knew how much she loved him, or at least how much he loved her. That's what mattered now.

But he let out a deep breath, and all his sad, nostalgic feelings faded away. He jostled his way into the food line with a smile on his face, and looked across to the crowd's favorite table. It had been shoved further down the room. In its place was a decorated booth. A bright red and white banner stretched from corner to corner saying SWEETS TO THE SWEET. Bart's smile widened — Kim's cookie business. He had almost forgotten about it. Kim was there taking orders while Woody stood nearby on a chair trying to drum up business. Business looked brisk, at least among the underclassmen. Woody spotted him and gestured wildly in his direction. Bart waved back and looked for Holly. Chris, Fiona, Jonathan, Dee, and Marc were at the table. Holly wasn't there yet.

"How do you guys do it?" Chris groaned as Bart walked up. He had loaded his tray with two jumbo burgers, fries, Coke, milk, and a wedge of chocolate cake.

"Maybe half's for Holly," Fiona suggested, moving her chair over and making room for him.

Bart chuckled. "No way. It's all mine," he said, shielding his overloaded tray with his brawny body. "Even if it weren't, she's not here yet so she doesn't get any." He faked a stern expression.

Dee giggled and grabbed one of Bart's fries. He grabbed another. "*En garde!*" he cried, and they began fencing across the table.

"*Touché!*" Dee cried, as her fry broke in half. She munched the other half and said, "Were you really expecting Holly to meet you for lunch?"

"Sure!" Bart said easily, then frowned slightly. He had the milk container halfway to his lips. He paused and asked, "Why? I mean, where is she?" He glanced up at the cafeteria clock. Holly was never late.

"Beats me," Dee mumbled through a mouthful of salad. "I haven't seen her since chemistry."

"Last time I saw her, she was headed out of the science building toward the parking lot," Chris interjected. "She was looking terribly mysterious about something."

"But we had a date for lunch!" Bart exclaimed, then clamped his mouth shut. His brow knitted up into a frown, and he slowly set down his milk. He had scarcely touched his food yet, but suddenly he didn't feel very hungry. He pushed his tray away and began uncrinkling the discarded wrapper from his straw. The scary feeling he'd had just now on the cafeteria line was back again. Holly had told him she'd meet him for lunch last night as they held each other one last time by the door. Bart shifted uncomfortably in his seat. Why was she heading for the parking lot after chemistry? Bart tried not to believe his next thought. When they had made up last night, she hadn't really told him much about that guy Matt.

"Hey, Einerson!" Jonathan bellowed from the far end of the table. "You look like you kind of lost your appetite. Feel like donating that cake to a worthy cause?" The gray-eyed student activities director poked his trademark Indiana Jones hat under Bart's nose.

"Ssshh! Don't bother him," Marc said in an exaggerated whisper, and elbowed Jonathan in the ribs. "He's worried."

"About what?" Dee asked, also in a whisper.

Woody walked up. He rested his hands on the table and looked around. He gave a meaningful wiggle of his busy eyebrows and pronounced, "Everyone's looking very serious. Somber. Even grave." He paused. "Has something *died*?" He cast a mournful glance at Bart's tray.

"No," Chris said. "But Holly seems to have vanished."

Woody rubbed his hands together. "A mystery! I love mysteries. Now where did Holly vanish to?"

"Good question, but no one knows the answer," Marc said, giving Bart a friendly shove. "What's the matter, Bart, you scared she's got a secret admirer?"

Woody clasped his hands together and batted his eyelashes in imitation of a silent movie star. "Clandestine meetings in the fog beneath the flagpole — how romantic!" he said in a falsetto voice.

Everyone cracked up but Bart.

"Bart doesn't like that idea," Fiona said playfully. She caught Dee's eye. They both started giggling. Fiona leaned over and twirled her finger in Bart's dark hair. "What's good for the gander is good for the goose."

Bart pulled away and glared at the petite dancer. Undaunted, she batted her big blue eyes at him. "After all that fan mail you get, why, it would serve you right if Holly had at least *one* other guy."

Marc and Jonathan burst out laughing. Chris tried to stifle a giggle and failed. Woody whacked Bart hard across the shoulder. "What's the matter, Bart? Can't you take a little razzing in the romance department?"

Bart clenched his fist beneath the table, but somehow he managed to smile. "All right, all right. The joke's on me!" He shielded his face with his hands as if to ward off a blow. He wasn't sure how to react but at the moment he didn't trust himself to say anything. All at once, it was painfully clear exactly why Holly had headed for the parking lot. Probably to meet that grease monkey again. Bart's throat was tight and his laugh felt forced as he pushed his chair back and got up from the table. "Well, the joke will be on me if I don't hit the books before next period." Again he managed to laugh, but even to his own ears his laugh sounded nervous.

Bart pulled up the hood of his raincoat and headed across the breezeway into the rain. He didn't know what he would say when he found Holly, but he couldn't stand waiting for her to turn up, walking into the building with another guy. He clenched his fist in his pocket and started across the grass. How would he face Holly if Matt was there? The idea of running into Holly with Matt stopped him in his tracks. Bart ducked beneath the roof of the breezeway to stall for time. Just then, the loudspeaker hanging in the eaves behind him crackled to life.

"Hello, Cardinals," a sexy voice breathed through the speaker. "This is Candy Hearts with your *Heartache Hotline*. Today's letter is from a girl who calls herself 'Perplexed.' " Paper rattled and Candy Hearts cleared her throat.

"Dear Candy Hearts,
I'm in love with a wonderful guy, and he loves me. He's kind, generous, and incredibly cute. The trouble is, every other girl in school

94

thinks so, too. When they flirt with him, he flirts back. He tells me not to be jealous. But I am. His flirting hurts. What should I do?
Signed, Perplexed"

"Dear Perplexed,
Honey, one thing's for sure, this guy doesn't know a good thing when he sees one. My advice to you is give him a dose of his own medicine!

Candy Hearts"

"Geez!" Bart cried, his voice getting swallowed up by the fog. Holly had actually written to Candy Hearts about stuff that was private between them. He was horrified.

Suddenly he was conscious of someone beside him. He looked down into Gloria Macmillan's heavily made-up brown eyes.

"Why, Bart Einerson, what are you doing standing in the rain? Is something wrong?" she oozed and put her hand gently on his arm.

Bart closed his eyes and counted to ten. "No, nothing's wrong," he said gruffly. "Nothing at all."

"Isn't Candy Hearts something else? Of course *everyone* knows it's Laurie Bennington. Pretty dumb of a girl to confide in her. That poor guy, he must be pretty upset. Don't you think?" Gloria tightened her grip on Bart's arm. The way she was looking at him, Bart realized Gloria knew exactly *who* "Perplexed" was. He looked away and focused his eyes on some imaginary point across the foggy quad. He had never felt so embarrassed in his life. If Gloria had figured it out, so had everyone else.

Gloria tugged Bart's sleeve. "No point getting wet, is there? I haven't had lunch yet, have you?"

Bart pulled his arm away and didn't answer. He strode off angrily down the path past the science building. Walking with his head down into the wind, he didn't see the slender figure in the bright green slicker coming toward him.

"Bart!" she cried.

Bart looked up. Seeing the hurt expression on his face, Holly took a couple of quick steps backward.

"What's wrong?" she asked, afraid to hear the answer.

"Wrong?" Bart cried. "How can you ask that? How could you do that, Holly? Write to Candy Hearts about us. Everyone heard and everyone knows that it's about me." He hit his fist against the slender trunk of a sapling cherry the juniors had planted last Arbor Day. His voice caught in his throat and she could tell he was very upset.

"Oh, I didn't think you'd hear it, Bart," Holly whispered, looking down at her hands. "But I really needed some advice and I wanted it from someone objective. I thought it was a good idea, and anyway, it's no secret that you flirt with all the girls. It's not like I let out anything new." Her voice trembled and she looked up, meeting Bart's eyes. He didn't look so angry now, just more hurt, disillusioned. Holly felt confused, but she didn't flinch or look away. Maybe writing Candy Hearts had been a dumb idea, but the problem between them was still there. It was real. She just wished Candy's advice had been different.

She hesitantly reached for his hand. "We can't stand like this in the rain," she said, gently pulling him toward a doorway on the side of the white brick science building.

Bart followed without protest. They stood awkwardly against the red door frame shoulder to shoulder, not looking at each other. The slight pressure of Bart's arm against hers reassured Holly, reminding her she loved him. For a long time they didn't say anything. Holly heard the tardy bell ring out across the quad. Neither of them moved.

"Where were you just now?" Bart finally said, moving away just enough so he wasn't touching her.

Holly looked up. "In the parking lot, listening to Candy Hearts on the car radio." She pulled a tissue from her pocket and wiped the rain from her face.

Bart eyed her dubiously. "Alone?"

"Of course," Holly said with an impatient toss of her head. "Why?" Her voice broke off. "Bart, are you going to start that again?" She pushed the damp curls off her forehead and planted her hands on her hips. "I wasn't with Matt Jacobs." She lifted her eyes to the sky and threw up her hands. "You're insulting. Did anyone ever tell you that? You just don't trust me and I've never given you a reason not to." Holly's eyes flashed fire.

Bart faced her head on. "You stood me up for lunch. What do you expect me to think — especially after yesterday?"

Holly didn't know what to say. She had simply forgotten. She had been so intent on hearing Laurie's advice alone, she had headed right to her car and eaten her sandwich and forgotten all about meeting Bart. "I forgot about lunch. I'm sorry about that. But I think you owe me an apology."

"I owe *you* an apology?" Bart sputtered.

"For thinking that about me and — Matt — " It felt strange to say his name aloud, coupling it with herself that way. " — and for the way you act with other girls. I've told you before, it hurts. It hurts at least as much as you hurt now picturing me with that guy." This time she avoided Matt's name. It made it less real, less important. The more she thought about it, the sillier Bart's reaction seemed — she had batted her eyelashes at Matt, smiled, and said, "see you around." That was all.

Bart didn't reply. He kicked at a loose stone in the path. Holly glanced at his face. A small vein in his temple was throbbing, his jaw was set, his head was bent. He looked so sad and tense. She longed to comfort him. She wanted to touch his cheek and make his face relax again, to tell him everything was okay. But she couldn't give in. Bart had to see what was going on and how unfair he was being. She pushed her hand back into her jeans pocket and waited, standing very still, almost holding her breath.

"I don't think you know how I feel about that

98

guy," Bart said finally. "And to tell you the truth, neither do I." He slicked back his damp hair with his hand. "I don't know what's happening between us right now, Holly, but I need a little time to figure it out. Okay?" he said in a trembling voice.

He held her glance for a moment longer. Holly almost believed he was going to kiss her, but he didn't. He turned around and started away into the rain.

Holly pressed herself back further against the door. "Will I see you this weekend?" she heard herself ask. Her voice seemed to come from far off, from another planet.

Bart stopped. He didn't turn around. His broad, proud shoulders looked a little stooped. He shook his head as if trying to clear something out of his mind. When he faced her, he looked confused. "I don't know. I'll call you."

Holly watched him walk a few steps down the path. He shook his head again, pulled up his hood, and broke into a run. She watched until his yellow raincoat disappeared into the fog. Then her shoulders sagged, and she leaned her head back against the metal door and closed her eyes. "What's happening?" she whispered, running her hands up and down her arms, remembering how it felt to have Bart hug her. She wondered what it would be like to never hold Bart again. Tears started building behind her closed eyelids. Something stopped her from running after Bart. He said he needed time to think things out. As the first tear slid down her cheek, Holly realized she did, too.

Chapter
8

Molly tried to ignore the herd of wildebeests thundering across the TV monitor at the front of the classroom. Even though Mr. Collins had said half the semester's ecology grade would be based on reports about the nature show, Molly wasn't in the mood to look at the graphic picture of survival on the Serengeti Plain. She wasn't the squeamish type, but watching a pride of lions tear a newborn wildebeest to shreds was upsetting her today. She felt too unsure, too vulnerable herself. She'd been feeling that way since yesterday, when she recognized Chris Austin in the girls' locker room.

Believing that Ted and Chris were back together had changed everything for Molly. Before spotting Chris, she had felt tense, energized, and nervous about her looming confrontation with Ted. Telling him they had to be just friends would have been a terrible thing, but the thought of just being around him again had somehow sustained her. And there had been the shadow of a hope he might talk her out of just being friends, that somehow she'd be able to let herself love again. But now her decision had been made for her.

Everything was different now. Molly felt all wrung out. She had barely been able to drag herself from class to class today. She wasn't worried about running into him in the halls anymore. Sooner or later it would happen. Kennedy wasn't *that* big. She didn't have to avoid him anymore. It would be awkward, but he wouldn't really care that she hadn't called him as soon as she got to Maryland.

As the credits rolled down the TV screen and a hum of conversation picked up in the room, Molly sat with her head bent over her desk, poking her pencil in and out of the spiral binding of her notebook. What if Ted didn't even want to be friends? What if seeing her embarrassed him? What if Chris got jealous? Molly looked out the window at the rain, and she suddenly felt Rose Hill was going to be a terribly cold, dreary place to live.

When the bell rang, she walked listlessly out of the room and bumped right into Phoebe Hall. At first she didn't recognize her. "Sorry," she mumbled and started to walk away.

"Molly?" Phoebe hurried after her. "Molly Ramirez, isn't it?"

Puzzled, Molly looked at the pretty girl with big green eyes. First she recognized the overalls. Then the thick red hair. "Oh, it's you — Shawn

Hall's sister," she said with an embarrassed smile.

Phoebe nodded and looked around uncomfortably. Molly had the impression she was afraid someone would see her, that Phoebe was doing something wrong. Molly pushed up the sleeves of her red V-neck sweater and stated rather than asked: "You go to school here."

Phoebe nodded. They were walking toward the west wing, where Molly thought her next class was held, although her schedule still confused her.

"I'm not sure where I go next," Molly said with a nervous laugh. "Want to help me out?" Phoebe was making her uncomfortable. She didn't seem like the same person who had come to the akido studio the day before. Yesterday, Phoebe had seemed alive and glowing. Molly had wanted to get to know her; she hoped they might become friends. But today Phoebe looked uptight. The stream of students rushing down the hall parted around the two girls as Molly stopped to rummage in her bag for her computer-printed schedule.

"You've got American history next. That's back the other way," Phoebe said, after looking over Molly's schedule. Her voice sounded strained.

"Do you have American history now, too?" Molly asked.

Phoebe shook her head vigorously. "No. I have French now." After an uncomfortable pause she continued. "But I'm glad I ran into you, Molly. I've been wanting to talk to you ever since yesterday." As the first bell rang, Phoebe steered Molly down the hall and up the back stairs to a cul-de-sac near some vending machines.

"I'll be late for class," Molly said, feeling Phoebe's contagious nerves. "We'll get sent to the office." Molly fought back a rising wave of panic. She had no idea why she felt afraid.

"Don't worry," Phoebe said. "We still have a few minutes."

She leaned back against the windowsill and swallowed hard. She picked at the frayed hem of her old Cub Scout shirt, then finally looked Molly straight in the eye. Phoebe ran her words all together, as if getting out what she had to say quickly might make it easier. "I-know-who-you-are-Molly. I-know-about-Ted. *About-you-and-Ted.*"

Molly felt as if Phoebe had punched her in the stomach.

"What?" Molly gasped.

"About last summer, and how you and he met at Ocean City — and what happened between you." Phoebe looked at her feet.

"How. . . ." Molly found her voice, "How do you know?" She was standing between the soda machine and the wall. Molly pressed her back against the concrete and braced herself for Phoebe's reply.

"Ted. Ted told me — "

Molly let out a small hurt cry and turned her face away.

"Oh, Molly, it's not what you think." Phoebe

impulsively took her arm. "Ted and I are good friends. We've known each other forever. People know there was someone, but he never really told anyone what happened but me. He needed a friend to talk to. Last fall, all winter. He told me so much about you," Phoebe said very gently.

Molly moved away from Phoebe and slid down to the floor. She hugged her knees to her chest and shivered. Staring straight ahead, not looking at Phoebe, Molly asked in a tight voice, "How did you know I'd be here, at Kennedy?"

"I didn't know until this morning. I saw you outside of my chem class. Then I saw you go into this classroom and I rushed back after my last class to make sure I'd bump into you," Phoebe said, then waited for Molly to respond.

Molly stared down at her white hightops. She had no idea what to say.

"Molly, why haven't you called Ted?" Phoebe went on. "I know you've been here a couple of weeks — at least since Shawn's class started — and Ted has no idea. He told me he thought he was going crazy — seeing you around Rose Hill. Why haven't you told him you're here? I know you haven't . . . because. . . ." Phoebe hesitated before continuing. "Someone's trying to fix him up for a dance and — "

"But what about Christine — that's her name, isn't it?" Molly said suddenly, her voice full of surprise.

"Christine?" Phoebe looked puzzled. Then she realized who Molly meant. "You mean Chris? Chris Austin?"

"Yes. His girl friend."

"Ted hasn't dated Chris since he met you. He hasn't dated anyone since you," Phoebe said very quietly. She took hold of Molly's arm. "Oh, so that's it!" She let out a long relieved sigh. "Molly, you thought they were still together — that's why you didn't call him. You couldn't possibly know — the whole time you were seeing Ted, Chris was seeing someone else, too. She's still going with him. His name's Greg."

Molly looked up. "The girl Ted told me about was dating someone behind *his* back?" She was astounded, confused, and oddly relieved. Ted's golden girl wasn't so perfect after all. All last night she had tried to imagine what Chris might be like. She went over in her head everything Ted had told her last summer: how Chris was wonderful but lived by a crazy set of rules that made him feel like he was in prison. Holly hadn't expected her to two-time a guy. Somehow that made Chris seem more human to her. Last summer Molly had the feeling she was competing for Ted's affections with some kind of perfect angel.

Phoebe hazarded a small smile. "Chris isn't the way she seems. I gather you've seen her."

Molly didn't answer. Her head was suddenly buzzing. She was so relieved Ted was free. But so scared again. Now she'd have to deal with either loving him, or learning to be just his friend. Both choices seemed pretty impossible.

Molly's next words startled Phoebe. "Have you told him I'm here?"

"Why, no. Not yet. I mean I just found out now for sure you were at Kennedy. I didn't know you were here until yesterday after I dropped Shawn off at akido. I remembered you from the raft race last summer."

"Don't — don't tell him," Molly said, her voice echoing through the empty hall.

"But he'll find out sooner or later — you can't keep hiding from him forever. Even if you don't love him anymore, you — "

"Don't love him anymore?" Molly gave Phoebe a puzzled look. "What makes you think that?" Suddenly Molly just wanted to digest this newfound information alone. She didn't want this stranger involved. "Please stay out of it, Phoebe," Molly cried, then buried her face in her hands. It was too much all at once: seeing Ted on the quad yesterday, resolving to talk to him, spotting Chris, now hearing Ted hadn't dated another girl all winter. He loved her, he still loved her. That made her happy and frightened all at once.

Phoebe stood by awkwardly for a second, not knowing what to do. Then she dropped to her knees next to Molly, and put her hand on her shoulder. "Molly, I'm sorry." Phoebe's voice was full of sympathy. "I didn't mean to make you upset. I really didn't."

Molly shook her head back and forth but didn't look up. She didn't pull away from Phoebe's hand. Part of her wanted to be angry at Phoebe, but she wasn't. She was relieved. Everything was out in the open now, and she'd call Ted this weekend. She had to do something. She couldn't pretend that waiting to figure things out would help anymore.

Molly looked up and pushed her hair out of her face. Her blue eyes looked very sad as she said, "It's not your fault. It's just hearing that Ted still loves me. It makes it all so hard."

"But why?" Phoebe asked, sitting back on her heels and pulling some tissues out of her bag.

Molly took them and blew her nose. "I'm not going to be here long. My mother's job only lasts until June," she said brokenly. "There doesn't seem to be much point in getting involved if I just have to leave again. It would be so hard. I don't know what to do."

Phoebe closed her eyes and sat very still. "Molly, it's not so easy just to tell yourself to stop loving someone. You can't just turn it off like that. You still have four or five more months before you'll be going anywhere. Why not just talk to Ted and see what happens?"

Molly looked intently at Phoebe. Suddenly she understood why of all of his friends Ted had confided in her. She was such a giving person. "Thanks, Phoebe," Molly said quietly, and stood up. "I'll think about it." She balled up the tissue in her hand, and cleared her throat. "And thanks for finding me and telling me about Ted. But please, promise you won't tell him I'm back."

"He'll find out sooner or later," Phoebe exclaimed.

"I know, but I want to tell him myself. I just need some time to figure out what to say. Promise?"

Molly searched Phoebe's green eyes. Phoebe sighed. "Okay. I won't tell him. But please," she begged, "talk to him soon."

"Don't worry. I will," Molly answered. Phoebe knew she meant it.

Chapter 9

Overnight, the rain had turned to ice and all the schools were closed. Holly was glad: She wasn't sure how she'd face seeing Bart in the halls and not being able to talk to him.

Her mother had gotten a ride to work with Bruce, and Holly was alone in the garage refinishing a bookcase she'd bought with Diana at a barn sale up in Maryville. The work was strenuous: Holly's arms were aching and she felt light-headed from the paint-remover fumes. But hard physical labor seemed to be the right prescription to keep her mind off Bart and the funny empty feeling she had inside.

She was sanding the last shelf when the Jeep pulled into the driveway. "Bart!" she cried, and peeled the rubber gloves from her hands as she hurried to the garage door. But it was Diana who hopped down from the driver's seat and waved. Bart wasn't with her.

"Hi! Thought you might need a ride to the clinic!" she shouted in greeting. Her high blonde ponytail swung behind her as she slipped and slid down the icy pavement to the garage door. She looked over Holly's shoulder at the piece of furniture Holly was working on. "Wow, look at that! Just last week that was a ten-dollar piece of painted junk." She picked her way through cans and rags, and ran her hand appreciatively across the smooth pale wood of the old-fashioned bookcase that Holly planned to put in her room. "Oak!" she said approvingly. She looked around the unheated cramped garage and tucked her hands back in the pockets of her down vest. "Brrr, aren't you cold in here?"

"Freezing," Holly admitted, hugging herself and wondering if Bart had said anything to Diana about their problems. "I was just about to break for some hot chocolate. I really had no idea how I'd get to the clinic. Dr. Ellerbee called and said to try to make it, but not to sweat it if I couldn't." Holly pulled her mohair scarf tighter around her neck. She tugged her old Irish fisherman's sweater down over her jeans and went through the door that led into the house. "Come on in."

"Bart told me," Diana said quietly, untying her red plaid scarf and draping it over the coatrack near the kitchen door.

Holly didn't know what to say. She filled a small enamel pan with milk. Her hand shook as she put it on the stove.

Diana hopped up on the counter top and swung her long legs back and forth. After a minute she said softly, "Holly, whatever happens with you and Bart, *we're* still friends. I want you to know that."

Holly faced her friend and let out a relieved sigh. "Thanks, Di." She folded and unfolded the potholder in her hands. "I was a little afraid, I guess. It's hard dating your best friend's brother." She tried to laugh but her face felt stiff and tight. She hadn't smiled once since yesterday. Last night she had been dying to talk to someone about Bart. But calling Diana had felt all wrong, especially since there was the chance that Bart might answer the phone.

Diana got up and spooned cocoa into some mugs. "I hate to say this. He *is* my brother, but he's not an easy guy for a girl to date."

"I know, I know," Diana added a little too quickly. "He said that he just needed space. I guess I don't really understand what happened. I mean, he's the one who's flirting all the time."

Hearing Diana say that gave Holly courage. "But Di, he doesn't understand how it affects me. I tried to tell him." She began pacing back and forth in front of the counter. "He just doesn't seem to hear. He keeps saying, 'It means nothing. It means nothing.' Then when I — " Holly cut herself off.

She pulled a stool over to the counter and sat down. She looked down into her mug. She poked at the marshmallow floating in her chocolate. When she spoke her voice was hardly audible. "Then when I flirt, just once to show him what it feels like, he acts as if I'm going to desert him."

111

Diana stared hard at Holly, then looked puzzled. "I don't understand. Since when are you the flirt? Bart's really beginning to lose his marbles. Don't tell me he's jealous!" She laughed a sharp little laugh. "I don't believe him. You know, he never mentioned that — *his* being jealous."

"He was — he is. Oh, I don't know." Holly got up off the stool and walked over to the window. The late afternoon sun was trying to break through the clouds. It was so cold the ice hadn't begun to melt yet. The whole world was sparkling but Holly didn't notice. She turned around to Diana and said, "I guess it's sort of my fault." She told her the whole story about Matt and the gas station and Bart's reaction and finally how, not knowing what to do, she impulsively wrote to Candy Hearts.

"Like Fiona said, what he needed what a dose of his own medicine," Holly concluded glumly. "The trouble is, he's acting like I gave him an overdose. He's really jealous and hurt, but to top it off, he's just too dense to see that I hurt whenever he carries on with other girls." Spilling all that out suddenly made her feel better. The tightness in her chest eased up. She still felt empty and hollow inside, but at least she didn't feel like she was hiding some deep dark secret. Suddenly she realized Diana hadn't said a word.

"Di?" Holly said, a note of fear creeping into her voice. Diana had stopped kicking her legs and was sitting very still. Her back was perfectly straight and a little stiff, and her kind generous

112

mouth was drawn tight and narrow. She seemed to be struggling to say something. "Is something wrong?" Holly asked nervously.

Diana met Holly's eyes. "Yes, something's wrong." She managed to sound controlled but she looked upset. "You were wrong, Holly. I can't believe you did that." Holly had never heard Diana sound so cool before.

"Write to Candy Hearts?"

Diana gave an impatient wave of her hand. "No, not that. Bart deserved it. He can't act like big man around campus after yesterday's broadcast. All the guys will razz him to death — and so will quite a few girls!" Diana bit her lower lip. "But that business with Matt Jacobs," she went on. "It was so — I don't know — how could you purposely do something like that? I never thought of you as a person who'd play games. As crazy as Bart is with girls sometimes, he never flirts with someone to make you jealous. He's not playing games with you. You know he'd never do that."

Holly's eyes widened. "I can't believe you said that! It wasn't like I intended for anything to *happen* with Matt, I just wanted Bart to see what it feels like. There was nothing dishonest about it. I don't see where the game part comes in." Holly's voice rose slightly. "And whatever Bart intends or doesn't intend, it hurts to see him watching another girl so closely when I'm around." Holly drummed her fingers against the sink. She suddenly felt so let down. Diana was her closest friend, and she was acting like Holly

113

had done something really wrong. Why had she bothered to confide in her? Now she felt miffed at Diana as well as Bart.

Diana got up from the stool and pulled the car keys out of her jeans. She obviously didn't want the conversation to go on much longer. Part of Holly wanted to let it drop before they got into a real fight, but part of her wanted to continue, to make Diana take back what she said about using Matt. She hadn't been using anybody. She hadn't been trying to *hurt* Bart.

They walked to the Jeep in silence. Halfway to the clinic, Diana picked up the conversation again. "I guess I understand why Bart is upset now."

Holly was about to protest, but Diana didn't let her. She quickly continued, "I believe you when you say he's got no reason to be jealous, but you can't expect him to understand that. Sure, he should shape up in the flirting department, but you have to work on things, too, Holly. You really are making too much of it. You have to learn to cope with Bart better. Playing games won't help. But he can't change completely. He'll always be cute, girls will always be after him, and sometimes he's going to flirt back. But I told you before, I know Bart's not going to leave you for some other girl — not unless you push him away."

Holly suddenly didn't want to hear any more. Diana's response surprised her. Instead of feeling better, she felt worse. Holly didn't know what to say to defend herself, so she made a big thing of staring out the window and rapping her fingers on the dashboard. She wasn't sure what she had expected from Diana, but she certainly didn't want to hear someone else telling her that what she did with Matt was wrong. The thought that she might have used him made Holly very uncomfortable, but not half as uncomfortable as the thought that her best friend couldn't understand her point of view.

As the low brick buildings of Rose Hill's medical clinic came into view, Diana cleared her throat. "Listen, I don't mean to sound so critical. It's sort of awkward, Bart being my brother and all. Maybe I can't be objective. I just feel you have to sort this out yourself, Holly. I told you what I think." Diana made a very careful slow right turn into the icy parking lot. She didn't sound angry, just frustrated at not being able to get Holly to see things her way.

As soon as she stopped, Holly opened the door. "Thanks, Di," she said sadly and hurried off. Instead of being soothing, Diana's advice felt like salt poured into a wound.

"What small-town post office in the continental United States is flooded every year with thousands of Valentine's Day cards?" Woody Webster stood in Kim Barrie's kitchen contributing to the commotion of the Sweets to the Sweet baking marathon by asking trivia questions.

Kim's pleasant round face scrunched up in a mock scowl. "Who cares?"

"Wrong. It is not Who Cares, New Mexico,

but Loveland, Colorado! One more point for me," Woody crowed and popped another heart-shaped cookie into his mouth.

Phoebe cracked up. "Is there really a Who Cares, New Mexico?"

Woody shoved back his tall chef's hat and pretended to tuck his thumbs under the suspenders that were hand-painted onto his T-shirt. Kim had bought him the shirt for his birthday. "Who knows?" he shrugged. "But at least it got you smiling again," he pointed out. He affectionately rumpled Phoebe's hair and looked carefully into her eyes. "You have been looking a bit out of it." He felt her forehead with the palm of his hand. "No fever."

"Woody, I'm fine," Phoebe protested and began furiously punching out daisy-shaped cookies with one of Kim's fancy cookie cutters.

"Well, anyone who looks like you do on the second snow day in the history of Kennedy High has got to be a bit sick."

Phoebe pelted Woody with a candy heart and went back to work. She didn't mean to look distracted, but she couldn't help it. She hadn't been able to stop thinking about Molly and Ted since yesterday. She felt terrible about upsetting Molly the way she had.

When Woody had turned up at her door, inviting her along to help Kim with baking her orders, Phoebe had been more than happy to get out of the house. Her father was doing all his business from home, hogging the phone, and Shawn was driving her crazy practicing akido in the middle of the living room, which made her think of Molly even more.

The cold and frosty walk to Kim's hadn't helped much. Woody had chattered the whole way, like he was chattering now. But Phoebe couldn't quite focus on anything. She couldn't forget how sad Molly had looked; how hopeless she had sounded. Now, rolling out cookie dough on the marble slab set in the counter of Mrs. Barrie's elaborate kitchen, Phoebe couldn't help but think that there had to be something she could do to help Molly — and Ted.

If only she hadn't *promised* not to tell Ted. She felt disloyal to Ted because she knew about Molly and he didn't. In spite of her promise, Phoebe had a feeling that talking to Ted would help. Ted would be over at Molly's house in a second. And once Molly saw him standing there at her door, she'd forget about tomorrow, and hurting, and there'd be no question of what she had to do. Molly had no choice but to love Ted. Phoebe knew that — she felt the same way about Michael. More to the point, Ted felt that way about Molly. But Phoebe wasn't one to break promises. If there were only something more Phoebe could say to Molly to help her make up her mind.

Kim pulled a tray of cookies out of the oven. "Perfect!" She beamed as she slid them off the cookie sheet onto a cooling rack. "Phoebe, you've got a knack with cookies!"

Phoebe smiled at Kim's compliment. "Thanks."

"Listen, I've got a great idea. Let me pay you for all the work you've done today. Tomorrow's the first day for delivering orders and if it weren't for the bad weather and you, I would have been in trouble."

Phoebe shook her head adamantly. "You can't pay me. I'm a friend, and this is really fun!"

"How about if I pay you with some cookies — a free Valentine's Day treat for Michael and for anyone else you want. I'll make it now, and you can take it home with the one you ordered for Shawn to give to his akido teacher."

Phoebe was about to decline and insist on paying for Michael's present. Then she had a brainstorm: "Kim," Phoebe began, "I give in. You can pay me. I'm still getting a cookie for Michael, and I'll pay for it." Before Kim could protest, she added quickly, "But I've got a really top-secret cookie to give to someone. I don't want anyone in the world to know about it," Phoebe said, shaking her pigtails earnestly. "So why not lend me your kitchen and take a break. I'll write my secret message on the cookie and put the box in the stack over there for Woody to deliver tomorrow."

"Phoebe Hall!" Woody pretended to be shocked. "You have a secret love and it isn't ME!!!!!" He sank in a mock faint against the refrigerator.

"It'd better not be you!" Kim growled playfully. She put her hands on Woody's knobby shoulders and marched him out of the kitchen in front of her. "Okay, Phoebe, Sweets to the Sweet is all yours. Just be sure that batch in the oven doesn't burn," she called out over her shoulder.

Phoebe didn't answer. She was already bent over the counter, her face screwed up in concentration. She held the decorating tool in her hand and slowly, carefully, squeezed out an icing message on a big chocolate cookie.

Chapter 10

The next day, Ted Mason entered his home-room feeling better than he had in weeks, like a great weight had been lifted from his shoulders. He did a couple of head rolls to stretch out his neck and slapped Marty Leonard five as he headed for his desk. Ted had a feeling something wonderful was about to happen. Not that he expected to fall in love again right away, but just deciding to take Carol Lacey to the Valentine's Day Dance had made him feel good again. Without Molly, the winter had been long and lonely and cold. Now it was almost spring. He felt restless and edgy in a good sort of way, the way he sometimes felt suiting up in the locker room before a big game.

He looked around the room for Peter. Before he spotted him, he saw the heart-shaped box in the middle of his desk. "What's this?" he cried.

"Come off it, Mason," Peter called from

across the aisle. "You can't hide your secret romance anymore. All winter long you've been moping around over some long lost girl friend — and now look at you. How long's this hot romance been going on?"

"Yeah, who is it, Ted?" Bud really razzed. By now, some more of Ted's teammates were gathered around his desk.

"Do I look like the kind to kiss and tell?" Ted responded good-naturedly. He was beginning to have his suspicions as to exactly who the valentine was from. Ted's Cardinal teammates were known for their pranks, especially when one of them got involved with a new girl. In fact, he wouldn't be surprised if Bart Einerson had put them up to ordering the cookie from Kim.

"So, will we meet her at the dance?" Marty Leonard asked.

Ted folded his arms across his chest and leaned back in his chair. "Maybe, maybe not." He caught Peter's eye and laughed. "In fact, I was about to ask Peter here for his cousin's number, but now, I'd better just check this out first. Right, guys?" Again he eyed his cronies, looking for a give-away grin. Everyone looked perfectly innocent.

Ted clumsily untied the huge red bow and opened the gold paper box. "This is great!" He slapped his thighs and chuckled. He proudly displayed the big chocolate heart to the crowd around his desk. *From a Distant Admirer*, the icing message read. Lying in the bottom of the box was a handwritten note. As Ted unfolded the piece of pink paper he realized the writing looked vaguely familiar. *Meet me at 129 Jefferson Lane in Georgetown at 5* P.M. *today*. It was signed, not love, but simply, *A distant admirer*.

A girl would have signed it *love*, Ted thought to himself. As Mr. Dillon began calling roll, Ted refolded the note and tapped it thoughtfully against the desk. I might as well go through with this, he thought. He'd head to Georgetown and check out whoever was waiting on the other end. The team probably had something crazy up their sleeve. Ted was always up for a good joke or two. Besides it was Friday, and tonight, like every Friday night for months now, he had nothing better to do.

Chapter
11

The bus for the planetarium was already parked outside the science building. It wouldn't leave for another twenty minutes, but Holly didn't care. When she walked up, the door was open, so she climbed in. The bus was still empty; the driver was nowhere in sight. The heat wasn't on yet and it was practically as cold inside as it was out. Holly chose a window seat toward the back. As she sat down and sighed, her breath came out frosty. Holly turned up the collar of her coat and tugged the sleeves of her sweater down over her hands. She had left her mittens somewhere — probably in the cafeteria, but she didn't feel like going back for them. She wasn't in the mood to face her friends. None of them had said anything over lunch. Everyone had tried to act normal, though Chris had cast a sympathetic glance down the table in her direction, and Fiona talked a little too brightly about the ballet class she had taken that morning. Everyone had noticed that she *was* there; Bart *wasn't*. They also saw Diana get up and leave not long after Holly had sat down. No, Holly definitely wasn't in the mood for friends.

She stared across the parking lot. It was a partly gray, partly blue day. Bart's Jeep was in its usual spot by the flagpole. The reflection of the midday sun flickered briefly against its polished green surface, then ducked behind another cloud. Looking at Bart's car gave Holly a funny feeling in her chest. She forced her eyes away and took a deep breath, then another. She threw her head back against the seat and studied the ceiling of the school bus. She had a heavy sensation behind her eyes, but she couldn't cry: Ever since her scene with Bart the other day, she hadn't been able to shed a tear. She felt dry as a desert inside and just as desolate. Holly felt as if the light in her life had blinked out, just like the sun right now behind the clouds. She tried to convince herself she was overreacting. After all, Bart and she hadn't really broken up. He hadn't said anything like that; neither had she. They were just taking a break from each other to think things through and try to figure out what was wrong between them. Today Holly was beginning to feel time wasn't what she really needed. The more time away from Bart, the worse she felt, and the less clear everything seemed.

A few students straggled onto the bus, and Holly purposely looked out the window again so she didn't have to say hello or talk to anyone. Her gaze drifted down the path leading to the main building. Lunch period was almost over, and the quad was buzzing with kids heading back to classes. At first she didn't recognize the tall, broad-shouldered figure cutting across the parking lot toward Kennedy's Little Theater. Her heart skipped a beat — it was Bart. She hadn't seen him all day, although she hadn't tried to avoid him. Holly just hadn't bumped into him, and she was glad because she didn't know how she'd act if she saw him face-to-face now. She pressed her hands against the frosty window to see him better.

The bounce had gone out of his walk and he was staring at the ground, kicking a stone ahead of him as he made his way through the cars. "Oh Bart!" she whispered aloud, then clamped her hand over her mouth. He looked so sad, so lonely. All at once Holly knew it was wrong: Time away from Bart wouldn't solve things. No matter how hard it was she would go out there now, tell him she loved him, and resolve to deal with their problems better. Problems had ways of being solved and she knew that together they could mend the differences between them. She stood up to get her knapsack from the overhead rack. She would have to go to the planetarium some other time. Right now, Bart was far more important than learning about the stars.

Then suddenly, Holly froze and sat down. Bart had stopped halfway to the theater. A familiar figure in a red rain slicker was running toward him, her dark, wavy hair bouncing in the wind. It was Gloria. Bart looked at her a minute, then began to smile his familiar, sexy smile.

His shoulders relaxed and he leaned back against the side of a pickup truck. Holly clenched her fist as she watched. She couldn't believe it. Leave it to Gloria Macmillan, Holly fumed. It seemed that Gloria did want Bart, and she certainly wasn't wasting much time. She put her well-manicured hand on Bart's arm and looked up at him with adoring eyes. Bart didn't pull away — he just stood there grinning. Holly felt sick inside. Diana had said Bart would never leave her for someone else unless she pushed him away. Is that what she was doing now? Holly couldn't watch anymore. She sank down in her seat, folded her arms across her chest, and looked the other way.

"Hi! This seat free?"

"What are you doing here?" Holly gasped, looking up into Matt Jacob's intense brown eyes.

Matt looked confused. "This is the bus for the planetarium, isn't it?" He glanced away from the empty seat to Holly and colored slightly. "Sorry, I guess you're saving this seat for someone." He looked around. Every seat nearby was taken. He started toward the last row.

Holly suddenly felt embarrassed. "No. Of course not. I mean, sit down, Matt." She picked up her knapsack to make room. He took it from her and shoved it on the rack, then shoved his black leather knapsack next to it.

He was taller than Holly remembered, though not as tall as Bart, and his knees looked a bit scrunched up when he finally sat down. He wriggled out of his coat. Only then did Holly notice the heat had been turned on.

"Aren't you warm?" he asked.

Holly realized she was. As she pulled off her pea coat, her hands were trembling. She caught Matt watching her and tried to smile. She wasn't sure if she was nervous because of Bart just now, or because Matt had remembered her from the other day. She wondered if he remembered her name. Suddenly she couldn't recall if she had even told him.

"So how come you're here?" she asked. She wanted to steer the conversation as far away as possible from any talk about the gas station. "Are you in one of Mr. Wylie's other astronomy classes?" Her tone was forced and light, and she doodled absentmindedly on the frosty window.

Matt shook his head in reply. "I don't take astronomy. There was a sign-up sheet in my homeroom — anyone could go if there was room — and I lucked out. Me and some friends are going camping in a couple of weeks down in the Blue Ridge Mountains. I thought it might be nice knowing what I'm looking at when I look up at the stars." His voice was gravelly and deep, but his dark eyes had a sad, soft look about them. Holly couldn't help but smile at what he said.

After a pause, he said shyly, "I don't believe I know your name."

Holly looked at him quickly. He met her glance directly and she had trouble looking away. Something about him was very magnetic. "Holly — Holly Daniels," she said, realizing she must not have told him before. She forced herself to look out the window. She didn't want him to think she was interested in him.

"Last time I went to the planetarium I was in third grade," Matt said. "They put the lights out for the sky show and I fell asleep." He laughed. His laugh was pleasant and reassuring. Holly began to relax. Matt was turning out to be a pretty sensitive guy. He hadn't mentioned the gas station and he didn't seem to be flirting with her. Matt must have remembered she had been with a guy. She knew he had noticed Bart when he came back to the car.

Holly remembered they were the same age. "What school did you go to before Kennedy?"

"Elmview."

"That's right down the block from where I live!" Holly exclaimed. She hadn't lived on the east side of town back in third grade. Before her parents' divorce, they had lived in a big, sprawling house not far from where Phoebe lived now.

"So we're neighbors." Matt's face lit up with a smile. "I've never seen you around the neighborhood."

"My mom and I just moved back to Rose Hill in September," Holly explained, then told him a little about her parents being divorced, and how she had lived in Baltimore. She found herself opening up to him easily. Matt seemed to be an intense, serious person, and very sincere. Holly was curious to know more about him. She sat cross-legged on the seat and turned toward him, listening intently as he talked a little about himself.

"My mom and I live alone, too — with my brother. He's twelve. But we've got tons of family around. There were probably even some Jacobs around back when Rose Hill was founded."

He didn't volunteer any information about his father. Holly studied him more closely — Matt had a lonely, hurt look about him. He was a guy who'd been through something. She instinctively wanted to reach out and help take the hurt away, but a thought flashed across her mind: Bart would probably think I was interested in Matt. She sighed deeply. If she hadn't been so impulsive with this guy in front of Bart, they could have spent a lot of time together — as good friends; nothing more.

Suddenly Holly realized she still believed she and Bart were going to make up; that everything would be okay. Even after that little scene with Gloria in the parking lot, Holly still didn't think of herself as not loving Bart. She turned her face back toward the window and pressed her forehead against the cool glass.

Matt's hand on her shoulder made her jump. "Sorry," he apologized, and hastily pulled his hand away. He stuffed his fists in the pockets of his denim jacket. "We're here." He nodded toward the round dome of the planetarium rising above a clump of pines across the road. He looked at her face and seemed about to say something. Whatever it was, he must have changed his mind, because he quietly handed Holly her knapsack and followed her off the bus without saying another word.

*   *   *

When the lights went out in the planetarium, Holly lolled back in the plush reclining seat and stared up at the blackened model sky. One by one the stars came out, and the resonant voice of the narrator almost seemed like an intrusion. Matt leaned over and whispered in her ear, "See why I fell asleep?" Holly laughed, grateful that Matt broke the mood beginning to come over her. Even watching fake stars without Bart next to her felt strange and lonely. "It's probably the same guy," Matt said in a loud whisper.

"Quiet over there!" Mr. Wiley called out from the far end of the row.

"Maybe he's a recording!" Holly whispered back. Matt cracked up and grabbed her arm. Together they laughed silently. Only after they recovered did Matt remember to pull his hand away.

Holly forced her attention back on the narrator. She had missed a good deal of his talk already. She had heard the same sort of lecture several times, but she always loved learning how the stars got their names. She watched the narrator's pointer dart from constellation to constellation. He paused a minute on Orion. Holly didn't quite catch what he said about the great hunter with his belt and sword, because looking at the grouping of stars she thought again of Bart. The weekend they went skiing he had showed her Orion. It was getting lower on the horizon because spring was coming. Bart had loved to watch the winter constellation from the meadow behind his family's ranch in Montana. Thinking of the look on Bart's face when he told her that, Holly forgot about the planetarium, the kids around her, Matt, everything, and burst into tears. She muffled her sobs in her pink mohair scarf. Holly didn't know if anyone noticed she was crying, but there in the dark, she couldn't stop.

Matt's hand was on hers in a second. He squeezed gently, she squeezed back. His hand was broad and calloused. Holding it, Holly felt suddenly grounded, as if she wasn't going to fly to pieces over Bart. Matt's other arm went around her shoulder. Slowly, gently, he ran his hand over the top of her arm and her back. She leaned her head against his chest and wept quietly. Her tears slowly died down but she didn't move away. Holly was incapable of moving. She felt emptied, drained, but very safe in the circle of Matt's arm.

When the lights went up, Holly and Matt didn't budge. Then someone snickered behind them, and they suddenly sprang apart. Holly blushed and bent down to grab her beret from her knapsack. She fiddled in the bag for a long time, trying to hide her tear-streaked face from Matt. Was she going crazy? What had she just done? She could still feel the warm, soothing touch of Matt's hand against her back. How could she tell Bart there was nothing between them now? Her heart stopped a minute. When she looked up her face was pale, her expression frightened. Matt had jammed his hands into the pockets of his jeans and had his gray scarf wound around his neck. He was waiting for Holly. They walked out of the planetarium in silence, and the whole way back on the bus they were very careful not to touch.

Chapter
12

Friday afternoon, Brian walked into the sub shop and grinned. The moth-eaten moosehead over the counter was wearing Jonathan Preston's felt fedora. Where Jonathan's hat was, Jonathan was sure to be nearby, probably with Fiona. Maybe Karen was there, too. Brian forgot all about ordering his Mean Mammoth Meatball sub and looked eagerly across the crowded floor toward the gang's favorite spot.

Before he saw Peter, the popular DJ spotted him. "If it isn't the *Soundings* man himself, Mr. Brian Pierson!" Peter's voice rang out over the general din. He sounded like he was introducing Brian on WKND over the campus loudspeakers. Brian was momentarily pleased with that effect. It was as if he had already won the new air-time contest, although he knew Peter hadn't decided on anything yet.

"All right! If it isn't the man himself!" Brian

good-naturedly boomed back. Shoving his hands in the pockets of his baggy trousers, and trying to look cool and calm, he slowly moved toward the crowd's favorite booth. He greeted everyone at the table with a wide, lazy smile. His eyes darted anxiously from face to face.

Monica Ford was there along with Peter, Michael, Phoebe, Brenda Austin, and Jonathan — but no Fiona, no Karen. His smile narrowed a little as he swung himself down on the bench next to Brenda and wondered exactly what to do next. He didn't want to let on that he'd been coming to the sub shop every day just to find Karen. She hadn't turned up once. She hadn't turned up anywhere Brian had been lately, in school or out. There was nothing left to do but call her. Charlie Walker's Georgetown jazz concert was tomorrow night. He'd have to get her number from Michael. He'd do it today.

"Dee, I'm starved!" Karen suddenly spoke up from the backseat of Dee's mother's Buick. She and Dee had just dropped off copy for *The Red and the Gold* at the printer's, then detoured to Georgetown to pick up Fiona after her Friday afternoon tap-dancing class.

"Ditto!" Fiona chirped in her British accent. "How about the sub shop?"

"All you skinny people ever do is think about food!" Dee groaned. She had recently lost thirty-five pounds and was proud of her new slender figure, though she wasn't quite ready to think of herself as a skinny person yet.

"Takes one to know one!" Karen quipped,

as Dee signaled to turn into the sub shop parking lot.

Dee angled the maroon sedan into a spot between Jonathan's pink convertible and an electric blue Trans Am.

Karen giggled as she tugged down her hat over her mane of hair. "Dee Patterson, couldn't you have chosen a color-coordinated parking spot?"

Dee blinked, then laughed. "You mean you don't like maroon with pink and blue?" She pulled her beret over one eye and struck an artistic pose. "And I thought I was the artist around here."

"Isn't this blue one Brian Pierson's car?" Fiona remarked, climbing out of the Buick, and holding the seat forward while Karen scrambled out.

Karen stopped, one foot in the car, one foot already on the curb. "Brian's here?" As soon as she said that, she caught Dee's eye and blushed.

Ever since running into him at the WKND studio the other day, thoughts of Brian had run through Karen's head like a dreamy sort of background music. She'd find herself scanning the halls between classes hoping to catch a glimpse of him. She never did. Their schedules were probably too different; she hadn't run into him all year, so why should she start running into him now?

Standing here now next to his Trans Am, she wasn't exactly sure she wanted to see him — especially with Dee around. Trying to keep her cool around Brian was going to be tough. Karen wished Dee hadn't figured out how she felt about him.

When Dee had called the other night to get a blow-by-blow description about her meeting with Peter, Karen couldn't help mentioning Brian. Of course, she didn't realize she mentioned him about twenty times in the course of the conversation — not until Dee pointed it out to her and insisted she had all the symptoms of someone falling head over heels in love. Karen had denied it vehemently, arguing that Brian was the competition, and not a guy she could ever think of getting involved with. She had a feeling she hadn't done a very good job of convincing Dee.

Well, Dee was here and so was Brian and there was nothing Karen could do about it. A hasty exit would only draw attention to her feelings for Brian. She pulled her hat off and tossed it in the back of the car. Fluffing her hair out, Karen smoothed her teal blue sweater over her tight black pants and followed Fiona through the steamy glass door.

"Just the woman I wanted to see!" Peter and Jonathan cried out together as the girls approached the booth.

Brian wheeled around. Karen met his eyes, then smiled past his shoulder at Brenda and the other kids. She felt the heat rising in her cheeks, and she was glad she'd worn her new sweater. While smiling, she quickly counted seats. Only room for one — two if they squeezed — in the already cramped booth.

"Gee, the booth looks pretty crowded!" she

heard herself saying. "Let's sit at the next table." She firmly grabbed Dee's elbow and pulled her toward a table directly across from the other kids.

Dee gave Karen an exasperated look. "Want to split something?" she asked, pushing her chair back. Karen nodded yes, but watched Brian out of the corner of her eye. A smile tugged at her lips when she caught him looking at her, too. Then he quickly glanced away and began fiddling with the tape in his Walkman.

"Like I was saying, I really wanted to see you!" Peter said to Karen.

For a second Karen almost forgot about Brian. "About the show?" Karen asked, amazed how calm she sounded. She turned slowly to Brian. His smile looked frozen. Suddenly she realized he was thinking the same thing she was. Her proposal had won. His had lost. Peter was about to break the big news. She tried not to look smug, and stifled an impulse to reach across and pat Brian's arm, to comfort him for losing.

Brenda interrupted Peter. "I bet you've got a ton of proposals now."

Monica groaned. "We're pretty swamped. Quantity, high" — she made a thumbs-up gesture — "quality, pretty low."

Both Karen and Brian relaxed slightly.

"I can imagine!" Phoebe rolled her eyes. "Everyone and his dog wants to be a DJ these days," she said, stealing a pickle from Michael's plate.

"Well, we're not just interested in another music show," Peter started.

Brian frowned. He drummed his fingers

against the table. Karen breathed a sigh of relief, then looked out of the corner of her eye at him. For another moment she felt sorry for him, but she couldn't help feeling happy for herself.

"I'm glad to hear that," Brenda said. She leaned forward earnestly over the table toward Peter. "I love your show — everyone does — but I think we need something else besides. Something more meaningful to the kids at Kennedy."

Dee walked up and set a Torpedo Delight on the table. She smiled loyally at Karen and said with conviction, "What Kennedy needs is a show like *What's News*."

Karen waited expectantly for Peter's announcement that he had chosen her show over all the others. Then she noticed Brenda leaning in her direction. "Tell me about your proposal," Brenda said.

Karen cleared her throat, and shyly began to explain what she had in mind for *What's News*. As she spoke, her voice grew more impassioned. By the end of her explanation she had the heady sensation she had convinced at least half the kids at the table that Peter just *had* to choose her show over all the others. She sat back happily, pulled a slice of ham out of the sub the three girls were sharing, and began to devour it.

"I think it sounds great!" Brenda exclaimed. "Maybe you could keep the student body posted on what's happening at places like Garfield House. And make regular announcements for community drives that need help: like the project to convert the old railroad station into a shelter for the homeless."

Jonathan seconded Brenda's feelings.

"I dunno," Brian broke in. "Seems to me people hear enough about problems on the regular news. I like the idea of a change of pace. Music tends to soothe the savage beast in us," he said smoothly.

Karen took his remarks as a challenge. "What you're talking about is escaping — behind those things!" She pointed to the earphones of his portable radio sticking out of his jacket pocket. "People deserve to be informed."

"But they also need space to cool out," Brian retorted. "That cruel world out there is drowning in its own information. Enough already. Sound's where it's at, not words. All that talk gets people into trouble." Brian banged his fist on the table for emphasis, then folded his arms across his chest and sat back in his seat. He looked Karen in the eye and waited for her response.

Karen stared at Brian. He talked more than anyone she knew. How could he pretend words didn't matter? Brian Pierson, you can't be serious, she thought. He couldn't really believe what he was saying. She was about to repeat her sentiments aloud when Peter broke in, gesturing for them to calm down.

"Whoa!" Peter shouted. "This isn't a one-on-one battle for air time, you know. You both have good proposals. In fact, what I wanted to tell you is that *What's News* and *Soundings* have both made the final cut."

Karen's heart sank. She hadn't won yet. The good news that she was still in the running hadn't registered.

Monica picked up the story. "We've spent the past two days — and nights — reading the proposals, listening to all the tapes that came in. We both have ear strain."

"A lot of the stuff was real junk," Peter continued. "But we've narrowed it down to four final contenders: Nicole Petersen from the Early Music Ensemble came up with an interesting program called *Unicorns and Flugelhorns*."

"What's a flugelhorn?" Dee asked, practically choking on her Coke. "Does it exist?"

"It's early. It's an instrument. Unlike unicorns, it does exist," Michael informed her solemnly.

"That makes three shows," Brian said with a frown. He had looked much happier about the idea of competing against just one show — Karen's.

"*Cloaks and Jokes*," Monica and Peter announced at once, then both cracked up.

"Sounds like a Websterism to me. I thought seniors couldn't compete in this contest," Fiona said.

"Woody swears he has nothing to do with it," Peter assured her. "Though it does sort of involve the Kennedy Players. Josh Ferguson's come up with a terrific idea, loosely based on some of the storytelling he loves on *Prairie Home Companion*. There'll be a weekly standup comic routine, a mystery, all sorts of stuff. He has it tied in with the literary magazine."

Karen groaned. An early music show sounded

140

like a bore, but *Cloaks and Jokes* sounded like something she wished she'd thought up herself. Everyone would love it.

Brian booed. "We're too old to listen to stories." Before he could continue, Fiona adamantly said, "Why, I'd vote for it if it were put to the ballot. I love mysteries. I love listening to stories on the radio."

"Sorry," Brian threw his hands up in a gesture of surrender. "I was only expressing my humble opinion. I'd prefer a news show to that." He glanced at Karen and she blushed. His expression was saying something she couldn't quite fathom. He looked slightly apologetic. She began to get the feeling Brian wasn't exactly sure how he felt about the competition between them, either.

"I'm afraid Fiona just stole my thunder." Peter faked a hurt look. "Now that the field's narrowed down, I don't think it should be my decision who gets this time. I spoke with the media advisor and he recommended we put the four shows up for a vote."

Karen sank down in her seat. A vote — all voting campaigns at Kennedy were notorious. If you could scare up a lot of interest, create enough commotion, anyone would vote for you, even if the issue were canceling weekends. Karen didn't have the high-power personality or know enough people to win any kind of contest. She had counted on the merit of her proposal to give her the spot. She believed in her news program wholeheartedly, but she wasn't sure she'd be very good at selling herself. Besides, students wanted just one thing — music. What they *needed* was something else, but Karen had no idea how she'd convince them of that.

"To make the choice easier, we're going to pre-empt my show on Monday and give each of you ten minutes to sell your show over the air," Peter said.

"Sell it?" Karen said. "You mean go on the air, just like that!" Brian arched his eyebrows and smiled again. His smile made her want to kick herself. She was scared of actually broadcasting, but she didn't have to publicize her fears. She clutched the silver amulet she wore around her neck and cleared her throat. "Actually," Karen forced her voice down to its normal range, "it is a good idea, and it's very fair."

"First you'll tell the kids what your show's going to be about, like you did in your proposal, then give a sample spot. Everyone will have the same amount of time."

Brian applauded Peter's plan. "What a great way to kick off a campaign," he said happily. His eyes glowed at Peter's suggestion. Karen knew exactly what he was thinking. Brian had a great voice, a magnetic presence, and he felt perfectly comfortable talking in front of people — probably in front of a mike, too. He knew Karen had never even seen a control board before she went to WKND a few days ago. In his eyes, the only real competition was probably Josh, who was a good actor and storyteller. He'd performed last summer down in Virginia at a folk festival storytelling competition.

At that moment, Karen vowed to give Brian

a surprise. She had the whole weekend to work out her show. She'd borrow Wanda's tape recorder. Maybe Wanda would even help her. Rehearsing with Wanda might get rid of some of her stage fright. Maybe Brian had the odds stacked in his favor, but she was going to give him some competition he wasn't counting on. The idea of competing with him didn't feel so bad anymore.

"No campaigning," Peter said firmly. "Nothing like that. Besides, there's not enough time. I want to get this squared away by next Friday. I'll just make the announcement about the voting on the air, and we'll have the art department make a poster. Ballot boxes will be outside the studio."

"Who'll keep people from stuffing them?" Karen asked, sounding a bit defensive.

"That's easy," Jonathan took over. "Peter and I talked about it this morning. We've gotten a list of all the students at Kennedy. He'll have it in the studio. Kids will have to vote during station hours. They'll come in, Monica and some other volunteers will check off names, give out ballots — one to a customer. It should work pretty well like that."

Jonathan rubbed his hands together and continued excitedly. "This should be really terrific. The winners will be announced next Friday at the dance. I think the school can use this right now — a little friendly rivalry. I hadn't thought of it until now, but did you realize there are two girls and two guys in the final running? That should spark some interest."

"Rivals?" Brian sat up a little straighter. He looked at Karen and the expression in his eyes sent a shiver down her spine. He wasn't looking at her as if he wanted her as a rival. Brian wanted something else. She held his glance until he turned away. Karen wondered if it was possible for rivals to be friends.

Chapter 13

Ted stood outside the entrance of the Georgetown Martial Arts, Fitness, and Dance Center with a puzzled look on his face. He leaned back against his red MG and tried to remember which of his buddies was into karate. He couldn't think of one. He peered into his car. The dashboard clock said 5 P.M. Once again, he checked the wrinkled piece of note paper in his hand. The address was right, 129 Jefferson Lane.

He shrugged his shoulders and ran his fingers through his hair. Who besides his pals from the team would send him a corny valentine? Woody Webster? No. That wasn't his style.

Jonathan Preston had a wacky sense of humor. Thinking of Jonathan, Ted remembered Fiona Stone. He snapped his fingers. That must be it. Jeremy's kid sister kept surprising everyone with her kooky sense of humor. Once she had gotten used to Kennedy and felt at home with the crowd, she had begun to show what Jonathan described as her true British colors. She was full of boarding school tricks. Only last month she had crept into the boys' locker room during fourth-period gym and stolen Woody Webster's suspenders on a dare from Kim. She turned up wearing them at the next day's music assembly over a pure white tutu. The whole school had burst out laughing as the tiny ballerina danced an entire *pas de deux* with suspenders on. It had to be Fiona who sent him the note and the cookie. Sometimes she took classes at the Center. He didn't know why she was teasing him with the valentine, but maybe Peter or Bart had put Fiona up to it. The guys had been on his case lately, egging him on about dating again.

He grinned a bit foolishly and started for the door. The mystery would be solved in a minute. He didn't know whether to expect Fiona inside, or a rowdy sampling of his Cardinal teammates. He hustled up the rickety stairs two at a time and braced himself for whatever awaited him on the second floor.

He had one foot on the top step when the studio lights down the hall went out. "Hey, come on," Ted groaned under his breath. Jokes were one thing, but this was getting out of control. He shifted his shoulders a couple of times and shook the tension out of his hands. Ted readied himself for one of his gang to jump him. He'd tackle them back, unless it was Fiona. A good-natured bearhug would do for her. Down the corridor, a red safety light was on over the EXIT sign at the far end of the hall. Otherwise it was dark. Ted could just make out the silhouetted figure bent over, locking a studio door. He took a couple of steps closer. It was a girl, but it wasn't Fiona. Beneath the dim light her hair looked dark, not blonde. She was sturdy like Fiona, but a little bigger and curvier, too. Ted's heart stopped beating for a second — she looked so familiar. He shook his head to clear it.

Whoever it was, even if his pals had put her up to something, he didn't want to scare her. He cleared his throat loudly. The girl looked up, startled. Ted gasped. Her face was thinner, her hair longer, but he recognized her instantly.

"Molly!" he cried.

At the sound of his voice, her hand flew to her mouth. She stood still as a statue for only a moment, then dropped her coat and bag — books, pencils, a makeup case clattered out. Molly didn't seem to care. She flew down the passageway into his arms.

Ted pressed her fiercely to him. She felt different. Thinner, not quite as sturdy as before. Her arms closed around his neck, and she hugged him so tightly it hurt. Ted lifted her up and swung her around in the narrow hall. Then he carried her over to the wall, and they slipped down to the floor still holding each other.

He pushed her back just enough to see her face. "Ted," she whispered. "You found me." Her round blue eyes shone with tears and were full of love, but they looked sad. Ted wanted to take whatever was causing the sadness away.

He put his finger on her lips. "Don't say anything," he whispered, his eyes drinking in every bit of her. She was wearing a red-and-white-striped T-shirt and worn, cropped white jeans. One of her red hightops had a hole in the toe. She didn't look dressed for winter. Ted smiled tenderly at that thought. He ran his hand up her leg, her side, and tilted her face into the light. The red glow cast dark shadows onto her smooth skin. Her lips trembled as he traced the outline of her flushed cheeks, her eyes. Then his hands strayed to her hair. "I like it long like this," Ted said to himself, suddenly not knowing the difference between what he was thinking and saying aloud. The large red barrette clamped around her ponytail popped open and clattered to the floor. Her curly hair bounced free and tumbled wildly around her shoulders. "Oh, Molly," was all he could say before covering her face with kisses. Ted didn't close his eyes as he kissed her. He was afraid if he did, he would open them and she would be gone again. She tasted sweeter than ever, and salty like she had at the beach last summer. Ted pulled back a little. "You're crying!" he said, surprised. Very gently, he wiped away her tears with the side of his thumb.

Molly took his face between her small hands and flashed him a huge smile that lit up her whole face. She looked happy and sad all at once. "You found me," she repeated.

Ted couldn't quite understand. "Of course I did," he whispered. He tenderly smoothed down the back of her shirt. "I got your note." He dug in the pocket of his jeans and pulled it out. It was wrinkled and torn. He smoothed it out before shyly handing it to her.

"Phoebe Hall!" Molly groaned and shook her head miserably from side to side. "I — I thought I could trust her. She sent you the note, I guess."

Ted tried to take in Molly's words. "Phoebe sent this?" Ted stared down at the note. The familiar writing — of course he knew it. It *was* Phoebe's. How did she get mixed up in this? "I — I don't get it. How do you know Phoebe?"

Molly drew her knees to her chest and pressed her forehead hard against them. She took a deep slow breath, and looked up. Her hand tentatively reached toward Ted's face. Then she pulled it back.

"From school."

"School?" Ted sounded really confused now. "You're going to Kennedy?" he asked slowly. He felt there was something he ought to be able to figure out. His heart was pounding and, with Molly sitting so close, he couldn't think very clearly. Molly at Kennedy didn't make sense. When he saw her running toward him down the hall he had pictured her running away from home, running the whole way from California back to him. Ted had reasoned this out as he looked at her. Then he realized Molly hadn't done that at all. It was too farfetched — like in one of his daydreams. Molly's presence was no daydream. She was really here.

Though they were barely touching, the warmth of her set his heart racing again. He reached for her. Molly carefully put a few inches between them. She turned and faced Ted head on. "I've

149

been in Rose Hill since the beginning of the semester. . . . I didn't call you because I didn't know what to do."

Ted's brow wrinkled. "*Know* what to do?" He shook his head in disbelief. "Molly, I still love you. All winter long — "

Molly put her hands over her ears and closed her eyes. "I know, Ted, I know. Phoebe told me you hadn't seen anyone else all winter long. Oh, Ted, it shouldn't have been like that. You promised me it wouldn't. When the summer ended, there were supposed to be other people. For both of us." Suddenly she jumped up and walked over to the banister. She leaned against it and folded her arms across her chest. She seemed to have trouble catching her breath.

Ted didn't move. Molly looked different than she had last summer when she was so care-free and happy. "I don't understand, Molly. What has this got to do with your being here? You're here now, that's all that matters."

"No, it isn't, Ted," she cried vehemently. "It isn't. I'm not here now, at least, not for long. It's all so crazy — " Molly broke off and turned her back on Ted. She leaned over the stairwell and peered down. When she turned around again, her face had a strong, determined look on it. Ted had never seen her look that way before. "Ted, my mother got a job here, but it's only tempo-rary, until June."

A look of comprehension crossed Ted's face. "You're only here until June," he repeated very quietly. He got up and jammed his hands down into the pockets of his varsity jacket. He walked down the hall a little way, then back again. He kicked at the baseboard with the tip of his sneaker. He looked at Molly with a sad smile on his face. "Four months!" The way he said it made it sound like four months was forever. "At least we'll have that."

"No!" Molly cried. "I can't do that again. I just can't." Ted reached for her. She slipped out of his reach and pushed herself against the wall. She kept her eyes lowered and began speaking very quickly. "I didn't wait for you all winter, Ted. I dated lots. There were a lot of other people."

Ted caught his breath. His hand closed in a fist, then he forced himself to relax. Of course, it made sense. Molly had said she had always lived like that. He had no right to be jealous, but he wasn't sure he wanted to hear the details. He lifted his hand and begged her to stop talking, but she continued, anyway.

"And it didn't matter. Everyone I kissed was you," Molly admitted miserably. "I've never felt this way about anyone before. I don't want to start up again, then leave in June, and have to get over you again."

Neither of them said anything for a moment. Ted stood very still, looking down at his hands. Molly fiddled with her hair and began looking for her barrette. Ted picked it up and gave it to her. His fingers closed around her hand. Molly tried to pull away. He didn't let her. He put his hands on her shoulders and gently made her face him.

"We still love each other."

Molly didn't look up.

"Last summer you said it was a summer kind of thing. You said we should live for the moment. Can't this be a spring sort of thing, Molly? Isn't loving each other all that matters?" Ted pleaded.

Molly dug at the floorboards with her toe. Finally she looked up. "Ted, I don't know anymore. I just don't know."

He let go of her and walked down the hall to pick up her things. His mind felt blank. Ted stuffed the pencil, the martial arts book, and the makeup case back in her bag before testing the studio door. It was locked. Molly handed him the key and waited by the top of the stairs.

As he approached she said, "I can't think with you here. I have to figure out what to do. It — it might be better if we just stayed friends." Her voice was so low, Ted could hardly make out the words.

He handed her her things. She slipped on her baggy cotton jacket and started down the stairs. Halfway down she turned around and looked up at him with her sad blue eyes. "Just give me a few more days. I'll think it out over the weekend."

Ted didn't know what to say. "Sure — I mean, I guess it's okay. Whatever you have to do." His voice sounded hollow and thin.

She locked the front door. Ted waited nearby, but he didn't walk her to her car. He watched her climb into the red Subaru with California plates. He watched until the taillights vanished down the block and around the corner.

The sun had set, the wind had picked up, and the temperature was dropping, but Ted sat down on the white wooden steps of the Center and propped his forehead in his hands. In a few short minutes, he had gone from being the happiest guy in the world to the saddest. None of it made sense. Slowly the facts began to register: Molly had been in town for almost a month and hadn't called him. He felt like someone had knifed him in the chest. Then he remembered how she had run to him, how she had kissed him, the incredible look of love in her eyes. The pain subsided.

He pressed his hands to his temples. He was so confused he felt light-headed. His hands smelled faintly of the flowery fragrance of Molly's shampoo. He could still taste her kisses. A tender smile crossed his face — today she had tasted like bubble gum, like salty bubble gum. Suddenly the whole memory of the summer flooded back to him. Molly in the waves, teasing him, chasing him, running away from him, surprising him with her akido moves. Molly eating cotton candy on the boardwalk. Sticky, salty kisses; sandy, sturdy legs. Laughing eyes that had a way of looking right down into the depths of his soul. That's why he had loved her then; that's why he loved her now.

"Molly Ramirez," he whispered to the empty street. "There's no way we could be 'just friends.' " Even as he said that, the smile faded from his face. The Molly he knew last summer wouldn't have been afraid of love. Something had changed about her. Ted dusted off his jeans and walked to his car. A few days ago the idea of Molly back in his arms had seemed so simple, so straightforward. Now Ted wasn't sure. Holding Molly felt incredibly right just now, but maybe she had a point. Saying good-bye would be harder this time around. Much too hard . . . and not just for Molly.

Chapter
14

"Last stop, Kennedy High! Everyone —
and everything — off!" The bus driver's com-
mand was met with cheers and hoots and jeers.

Matt and Holly were all the way in the back.
"Wait," he said, "until the crowd thins out."

Holly didn't want to wait. She wanted to get
out into the cold night air, get into her car, and
drive home. She wanted to get away from Matt.
The whole way home, they had been careful to
leave a space between them on the narrow bus
seat. Still, Holly could sense the warmth of
him against her body. She blushed slightly, remembering how safe and secure she had felt in
his arms in the planetarium. When the lights had
gone up, she had almost forgotten where she
was, why she had been crying. In Matt's arms
her heartache over Bart had almost seemed like
a distant bad dream. When the show was over,
the dream was back. It was worse now, because

Matt was really part of it. That thought frightened her, so she wanted to get away from him as fast as she could.

But she had to wait, anyway. The kids were slow grabbing the stuff off the racks and the aisle was jammed. She couldn't run anywhere.

"Are you busy now?" he asked, pulling his black leather knapsack off the rack.

"I've got to go," Holly said, struggling into her coat. Suddenly he was holding it for her. His gesture confused her, like everything else about him. He seemed so rough-edged, but he was polite and gentle.

She climbed down from the bus first. "Goodbye," she said quickly, not turning around to meet his eyes. Holly sensed that spending any more time with Matt would be the wrong thing to do. She felt drawn to him — she had a feeling she could tell him everything and he'd help her understand what was going on. But telling him about Bart seemed like betraying a confidence, revealing a secret, breaking a promise. She knew Bart wouldn't understand if she talked to Matt, or went somewhere alone with him. Holly pushed her hair back from her face and started for the car.

Matt didn't say good-bye. He walked right behind her across the lot, not saying a word. His workboots squeaked against the tarmac. When she tried to put her key in the lock, he blocked her way. He said very softly, "Holly, do you want to talk?"

He wasn't speaking loudly, but Holly jumped. "No!" she practically shouted. "I mean, everything's okay, Matt. Really. But thank you," she added, meeting his glance this time. It was dark where her Malibu was parked, but she could still see the look of concern on his face. She let out a long, slow breath. It wasn't his fault she was feeling confused. It was just that everything was such a jumble and somehow Matt had become part of it. She looked down at her hands. She was twirling her key chain around and around. If only things were different, Matt could be just the kind of friend she needed right now.

"I was thinking we could have dinner together. We could go somewhere for a little while, eat, talk. It's Friday night."

Holly looked past Matt's shoulder. Very few cars were left in the lot. The spot near the flagpole was empty. Bart's Jeep was gone.

"Yes, it is Friday, isn't it?" Holly said, surprised. She had forgotten all about the weekend. Not counting Christmas vacation, when Bart had gone to Montana, this was the first Friday since November she hadn't spent with him. She pictured herself sitting home alone in her room, knowing the phone wouldn't ring, not even able to talk to Diana. The house would be empty; her mother would be at Bruce's. She shivered unconsciously.

"I guess it would be okay," she said, more to herself than to him. Then she looked up and said a little louder, "Sure, dinner would be fine, Matt."

When Matt steered his old pickup truck onto the Interstate, Holly breathed a sigh of relief. In the fifteen minutes between the Kennedy parking lot and downtown Rose Hill, Holly had had about a million second thoughts about going somewhere alone with Matt Jacobs. What if he wanted to go to Mario's or the sub shop? What if someone saw them together? That's all she needed now to top off her problems with Bart. He'd never believe anything she said again. But she'd been too shy to ask Matt to avoid the usual hangouts. How could she explain she was scared to be seen out on a Friday night with someone who was just a friend?

Matt drove a little way south into the Virginia countryside. The landscape darkened as well-lit suburban communities gave way to the first farms. Holly hadn't driven down this way since she was a kid and had gone to Williamsburg on a fifth-grade day trip. She pressed her nose against the window and almost gave a cry of delight as Matt signaled and exited the highway at a truckstop. The towering yellow-bordered sign spelled out TRUCK STOP, one pink letter at a time, then flashed the gaudy neon words agaist the dark sky three times.

"I haven't been to one of these since I drove to Florida with my mom four years ago," Holly said as Matt pulled into the lot and parked between a couple of big rigs. She turned to face him, her eyes shining.

Matt's face lit up with pleasure. He didn't take his eyes from Holly's face as he said, "I'm glad you don't mind. Sometimes I like coming out here. It's a change from the scene back in town."

A change of scene was just what Holly needed. Sitting there with Matt, the country music station blaring across the tacky dining room, she began to relax. The bright lights made all her crazy feelings seem unreal. The low buzz of truckers' conversation filtered over toward them. How the weather was a few days back in Nevada. Diesel prices down near Atlanta. Speed traps on the Interstate ten miles south of here. Some driver mentioned a snowstorm closing part of I-94. Holly's ears perked up. I-94 went through Montana. Bart had pointed it out to her on a map once. He was showing her where Superior was, the closest town to his family's ranch. Population: 225. She wondered if it was snowing there.

She let out a long sigh. Thinking of snow in the Rockies and Bart on his ranch sort of put things in perspective again. For the past few days her world had narrowed. She had barely thought of Bart as Bart: the warm, expansive guy she loved. She had begun to see him as just a flirt. A macho guy. A football hero. Mr. Popularity. Holly ran her fingers through her hair and stretched her head back. Fake brass lanterns swayed in the current from the ventilating system. She felt mesmerized watching the glass baubles twinkle above her head. Maybe Bart had been right — maybe time would help. Time and space and a little bit of distance. The quad, the pep squad, and Bart's popularity contest seemed pretty unimportant right now. Kennedy High wasn't the whole world. Bart had often told her that. Holly suddenly got an indefinite, hazy feeling that her problems with Bart would pass. Their love was bigger than anything.

"This place seems to agree with you." Matt smiled at her over his Coke. Only then did Holly realize she was smiling, and that since they arrived at the truck stop she hadn't said a word.

She felt she ought to apologize for being here with Matt, spending all her time thinking about Bart. She said the first thing that came to her mind. "You were right, sometimes a change of scene does help." She looked down at the table in front of her. From somewhere a burger had appeared — a deluxe burger with fries. For days now she hadn't been hungry, but suddenly she was ravenous. Holly looked back up at Matt. She got the feeling being with him had something to do with making her let go of her bad feelings.

"So, do you want to talk about it, what was bothering you today in the planetarium?" Matt asked outright.

Holly was taken aback. She put her burger on her plate and shook her head no. The happy feeling from just a minute ago had vanished.

Matt leaned his elbows on the table and propped his chin in his hands. "Do stars always make you cry? Remind me not to take you to see *Star Wars*," he joked, but his eyes stayed serious and concerned.

Holly didn't laugh. She looked down and studied the placemat. It was one of those cheap white paper ones with badly printed games to play: See what word is spelled wrong, connect the dots, find the hidden animals, complete the square without taking your pencil off the paper. Looking at the placemat made it easier to talk, but even as she talked she surprised herself. She hadn't planned on confiding in Matt, but all along she had needed someone to talk to, someone who'd listen.

"This may sound really dumb," she started with a nervous laugh, pulling apart the inside of her hamburger bun. "I've got trouble with this guy. I've been going with him a long time — four or five months now. He's incredibly handsome and every girl at school seems to notice him." She stabbed at the placemat with the prongs of her fork. "The trouble is, he flirts with almost all of them and it gets to me sometimes." Admitting that made her feel better; it also made her afraid Matt would think she was the jealous, possessive type. That thought bothered her tremendously. She had never seen herself that way before.

"It would get to me, too," Matt said. "But some guys are like that. It's part of their image."

"That's what he says. He says it means nothing, but when I — " Holly cut herself off. All of a sudden, she was blushing furiously. Telling Diana about flirting with someone was one thing, but she had just almost spilled the whole story to Matt.

"Was he the guy with you at the gas station the other day?" Matt asked. He didn't sound judgmental. Suddenly she realized he probably knew Bart, at least by sight. Everyone at Kennedy did.

Holly cringed, but she nodded yes.

"If I were with someone like you, I wouldn't know any other girl existed, but I'm a different sort of guy."

From anyone else, it would have sounded like a line. From Matt, it wasn't like that. Holly knew Matt wasn't a flirt. She could tell from the way he looked at her that he liked her, and it scared her a little. He wasn't trying to act like a big man around town or con her into feeling sorry for him — none of the usual things guys did to impress a girl. Again Holly had a sudden desire to really be his friend, and with that thought she blushed again. If Matt had the wrong idea about what she wanted from him, it was her fault. She wanted to kick herself for flirting with him. She wondered dismally if she had screwed up all chances for a plain and simple friendship. A distant warning bell went off in her mind: Something about this evening didn't quite feel like friendship. All day long, and even now, something almost kept happening between her and Matt. She didn't quite understand what. She wasn't trying to lead him on in any way, but she felt drawn to him so strongly it confused her.

Matt reached across the table and took her hand in both of his. Holly caught her breath but didn't pull away. She was afraid to move, afraid to look up. "Matt," she said, her throat suddenly going dry, "I —"

"Holly, look at me." The way he said it she had to obey.

She swallowed hard and looked up into his

dark eyes. She couldn't quite make out his expression. In the background, Waylon Jennings crooned a sad tune. Holly was glad she couldn't hear the words. She knew it was a very romantic song.

"If you love this guy, you've got to be honest. With him, and with yourself. You have to live with it the way he is, if you can. If you can't — " Matt didn't finish. He looked down at his hands holding Holly's and let go. He went back to fiddling with his napkin. A hint of color flushed his cheeks.

For the second time that day, Holly noticed how attractive he was. Not in a bigger-than-life way that you noticed right off the bat the minute you saw him, but in a subtle way that took getting used to. His nose was a little crooked and his face was very smooth. There was a small scar near his right eye. His eyes were large and very kind, and they seemed to pierce right through her. No one else had ever looked at her that way before, not even Bart. Something about Matt was more complicated than Bart but Holly couldn't figure it out. She only knew that although he didn't know her at all, he understood her. She caught herself staring at him and forced her gaze across the room.

After a second, Matt cleared his throat. He pushed back his chair, and ran his fingers around the collar of his T-shirt, as if it were too tight, like a tie. "It's funny we haven't run into each other before. Which kids do you know in school?" Holly realized he was purposely

163

changing the subject. They talked about Kennedy, the Fix-It Club that Matt had started last fall. He told her about his work at Garfield House with Brenda Austin.

Holly wasn't following what he was saying. She was trying very hard not to look in his eyes. She began getting the feeling they were carrying on another conversation on a different level that had nothing to do with words. The more they talked, the more she felt things were being said that had to do with the loneliness she felt inside.

She wasn't sure when he asked for the check. She hardly remembered the long ride back to school to get her car. Only the static of a blues station fading in and out of the pickup truck's AM radio reached her clearly. Holly asked Matt not to take the Interstate. She wanted the ride to last longer, the car to go slower, to watch the shadow of the pines fall across the two-lane highway. She told him what she knew about astronomy and the waning moon. It was high in the sky now and still bright.

They pulled into the parking lot and Matt walked her to her car. As Holly turned around to say good-night, she knew exactly what was going to happen. The cold, dark night had made her so lonely she didn't fight it anymore. Matt kept his hands in his jacket pockets but leaned toward her. He waited a second as if to give her a chance to change her mind. Holly was afraid to move. Then he brushed her lips with his. It was an incredibly gentle kiss.

She stared up at him and gazed into his eyes

a long time. She was confused and puzzled and she felt like kissing him again. She didn't resist this time as his lips found hers in the dark. This kiss lasted longer. His arms circled her waist and she rested her cheek against his chest. Against the delicate skin of her cheek the smooth denim of his jacket felt rough. His heart was beating strong and slow and she almost felt hypnotized listening to it. She lifted her face toward his, longing to read in his eyes what he was feeling and thinking at that moment. His dark head bent once more toward hers and they kissed again. She didn't feel the sparks she felt when she kissed Bart, but she couldn't help responding to his touch. Holding him like this made the emptiness inside her seem to vanish. When he stopped kissing her, the bleak, hollow feeling came back stronger than ever. His body pressed against hers and the door handle of the car poked her in the back. He moved away from her slightly and cupped her face in his hands. Holly looked at him. His dark eyes reflected the moonlight bathing the car, the pavement.

A siren wailing in the distance broke the incredible silence around them. Holly blinked and everything was suddenly in focus, sharp and clear.

Matt wanted her to love him and Holly knew she couldn't. She loved Bart. Matt's kisses couldn't change that. She closed her eyes and turned her face away. She suddenly knew that this was all wrong. Thinking of Bart somehow snapped her to attention. "No, Matt," she whispered, "I — I can't. I have to go home. This is wrong." She didn't trust herself to explain just then.

Matt stepped aside. Holly's hand shook as she opened the door. She turned around and again looked him right in the eye. "Thank you, Matt, for dinner — for everything." Her husky voice was barely audible and Matt bent closer to hear her.

She climbed in the car and rolled down the window. Matt's hand strayed to her face. Very tenderly he brushed away the curls from her forehead. "See you around?" he asked in an uncertain voice.

Holly didn't know how to answer. She kept her eyes focused on the windshield and flicked on the ignition and her headlights. A minute later she was driving down the boulevard trying to sort out the incredible jumble of feelings rolling around inside her. Her hands were shaking and her eyes were blurry with tears. She drove the few blocks down to the sub shop and pulled into the deserted lot. She left the engine running, but turned off the headlights and pulled on the handbrake.

She leaned her head against the steering wheel and sobbed. She wasn't sure what was happening to her. She thought of holding Matt, her feelings for Bart, for Matt, all her fears about losing the guy she loved. Everything that had been pent up inside her for days now came spilling out. She had a terrible feeling she had just ruined everything. Why had she let Matt kiss her like that? She didn't love him — she didn't even know him.

Holly sat very still and digested that fact. What she felt with Matt was safe and secure, the kind of thing friendship was made of; not love. Holly's stomach plunged to her feet. Holding Matt like that had taken her loneliness away. That's why she hadn't stopped him. Holly had been using him so she wouldn't miss Bart. Holly shuddered. She didn't want to think about what Diana would say about her now. This time she might be right. Holly wiped her arm across her nose, and reached into the glove compartment for some tissues. She shook her head dismally. What had she just done?

She leaned her head against the seat and rolled down her window a crack. The chill night air cooled her burning cheeks. Slowly her tears subsided. All she had done was kiss a guy she shouldn't have been kissing. Holly felt terrible about that, because of how Bart would feel and because of what Matt might think. Holly had only kissed him because she was lonely and scared and confused.

She remembered the look in Matt's eyes and suddenly knew what it meant. He liked her. He knew about Bart and wasn't going to push anything. Matt would just wait and see what happened.

Holly sat up straight in her seat and decided then and there, she had to stop seeing Matt now. Things had to be straightened out with him before they got out of hand, before she really hurt him. She would find him on Monday and tell him that tonight had been a mistake. She loved Bart and no matter what it took, she'd find a way to make that love work again.

The old pickup truck turned off Cherry Street and onto Lincoln. Halfway down the block it pulled over to the curb. The headlights flicked off. Matt Jacobs climbed out into the silence of the early hours of the morning. He stretched his wiry muscular arms high above his head and stared over the roof of Jonathan Preston's house to smile at the moon. The round attic window on top of the three-story house was dark. Even Jonathan's mother had quit her typewriter for bed.

Matt ignored the slatted gate and vaulted over the low white picket fence into the front yard. He moved toward the side of the house. Looking up to a window over the porch, he let out a low whistle. From inside the kitchen came a growl, then a cautious bark. "Shut up, Sherlock, it's me!" he said in a low, firm voice. The dog whined in recognition, scratched at the doggy exit in the bottom of the back door, then settled down. When Matt whistled a second time, Sherlock remained silent. Matt scooped up a handful of gravel from the driveway and began pelting the second floor window with pebbles. A second later the window flew open and Jonathan Preston poked out his head and shoulders. He was wearing a striped pajama top.

His sleepy face lit up with a smile. "Matthew

Jacobs! Do you know what time it is?" he asked in a loud whisper.

"One-ten and fifty seconds!" Matt replied, leaning back against the gnarled trunk of the old apple tree.

Jonathan shook his head in disgust. "What's up?" he asked with a yawn.

"'Feel like taking a walk?"

Jonathan grinned and ducked back in the window.

Matt sat down on the swing that hung from the thick, strong branches and twirled the seat around and around, then let the ropes unwind again. The grass was worn away beneath the swing, and he kicked at the bare circle of dirt with the scuffed toes of his boots. The tune to "Georgia" was running through his head; he began to sing it softly in his deep gravelly voice, sounding like a cross between Bob Dylan and Willie Nelson. It had been playing at the truck stop tonight and he hadn't been able to get it out of his head. He took a little jog around the tree, then hopped back on the swing and began pumping it with his powerful legs. Soon he was flying almost as high as the porch roof. He stopped pumping, and when the swing slowed a little he jumped off, hurling himself onto the frozen grass. He landed with a thud, then threw himself down on his back and looked up at the stars. He knew the name of one more constellation now: Orion.

Five minutes later, Jonathan's coat came flying out of the second floor window. Matt sprinted toward the house and caught it in midair. Jonathan eased his long legs onto the shingled roof and scrambed down to the ground. Without saying a word the two boys headed across the yard and over the back fence, Jonathan in his wool overcoat, Matt in his thin denim jacket.

Jonathan didn't ask where they were headed or why. He didn't have to. Whenever Matt or he needed to talk, they'd go on one of their midnight rambles down the back streets of Rose Hill, stopping either at the abandoned railroad station or on the other edge of town near the industrial strip that bordered on Carrolton. They had been taking walks like this since they were twelve years old. They had been best friends ever since they'd met in day camp. Matt hung out so much at the Prestons' he had practically become part of the family. Jonathan's dad had become a substitute father to him; Matt's own dad had left his mom when he was eight, and neither of them had seen or heard from his father since.

The ritual was always the same — Matt would turn up in the early hours of the morning and Jonathan would scramble off the roof. They'd prowl the dark streets enjoying the silence and the excitement of doing something that felt dangerous and out-of-bounds.

Tonight they headed for the strip. Jonathan shivered slightly in his warm coat, but Matt didn't seem cold at all. Every so often he'd stretch his arms open to the wind, throw his head back and grin. There was a new bounce in his walk and he was charged with a nervous energy, swinging round lamp posts, and jumping up every so often to touch the bottom of a sign with the tips of his fingers.

Neither boy said a word until they neared the back of a construction site at the edge of a small shopping center. Matt led the way, squeezing through an opening in the chain-link fence. Pale yellow light from the back windows of the all-night diner spilled out onto the blacktop.

"You know Holly Daniels," Matt stated rather than asked.

"Sure, Bart Einerson's girl friend. You know him from around school. He's — " Jonathan broke off. Suddenly Matt's good mood, the time of night — everything began to make sense. "Why?" he asked cautiously.

"I met her today at the planetarium," Matt said. After a pause he added, "You sure about her and Bart?" Something in his voice confirmed Jonathan's suspicions.

They were on the bottom step leading to the brightly lit diner. Jonathan then hoisted himself up on the black iron railing. "Forget it — she and Bart have this big thing going," he warned.

"Don't be too sure of that," Matt said, grabbing the railing with his hand and leaning way back.

Jonathan looked across the lot and turned up the collar of his coat. He shoved his hat back and rocked back and forth on the narrow rail. A couple of small trucks were parked in front of the building. Otherwise the lot was deserted. An Elvis Presley song seeped out under the closed, steamed-up doors. Jonathan had heard Holly and Bart were having trouble. Everyone had noticed. Bart had turned up solo at Rose Hill Bowling Lanes tonight, and no one had seen Holly since lunch.

"Matt, she's not available — believe me."

"That's not the impression I got," Matt said a bit gruffly, then shut his mouth. He hadn't meant to say that. What had happened between him and Holly wasn't Jonathan's business. He didn't want anyone talking about her that way, getting the wrong impression. Holly was such a special person.

Matt walked away a bit and propped himself against the pole of the bright DINER sign. Maybe he shouldn't have mentioned anything to Jonathan, even though he knew he could trust him not to say a word about it. And even if Holly or Bart were his close friends. Talking to Jonathan had taken the edge off Matt's incredibly joyous mood, but no matter what Jonathan said, Matt still wasn't sure about Holly and Bart. Not after his talk with her tonight. Hearing that Bart treated Holly the way he did made Matt angry. He hadn't needed Holly to tell him; he had noticed something was wrong that day at the gas station. He could tell Bart didn't mean anything serious by flirting with that girl, that was just his way. Matt couldn't imagine treating any girl like that, especially a girl like Holly. She was the kind of girl that Matt had always dreamed of: soft, gentle, and beautiful in a fresh sort of way.

Holly was the kind of girl he never dreamed would like a guy like him. He thought of himself as too rough-edged, uncultured. When she had smiled at him in the gas station the other day, he had begun to hope. Running into her on the bus had seemed like fate. And she had liked him — she really seemed interested in who he was, and what he had to say. He had almost started talking about his home, his family, his dad. The only person he ever had talked to about that was Jonathan. But he had stopped himself from telling Holly. She was too upset; she was hurting. And Holly was the one who needed listening to tonight, not Matt. He wasn't ready to give up yet.

Jonathan's voice broke the silence. "So, are we going in?" he said, sensing their talk had ended.

"Sure." Matt strode up the steps. He and Jonathan faked a few punches just outside the door. Matt's laughter broke the subtle tension between them. He was laughing because Jonathan hated violence. He couldn't fight to save his life, and even faking punches looked as unnatural to him as being without his hat.

"Who's treating?" Jonathan joked when they sat down, emptying his pockets on the table. He waved two dollars in Matt's face. It was another part of their ritual. They'd pool their money and get the hugest breakfast they could afford.

Matt produced a single and some change. He had forgotten that he had bought Holly dinner.

Matt looked woefully at Jonathan. Jonathan mugged a gloomy face. As the waitress approached, they both said at once, "Two budget breakfast specials."

Chapter
15

"Hello out there, Cardinals! This is Karen Davis with today's premiere edition of *What's News*. In the next ten minutes you'll hear a sampling of news, views — everything that pertains to *you* as a Kennedy High student."

"Ugggghhhh!" Karen cried and tossed the tape recorder microphone down on her desk. She stomped over to her desk chair and sat down with a thump. "That's the dullest thing I've ever heard!" she said. "*I* wrote it and I'm putting myself to sleep listening to myself read it!"

She picked up the sheaf of neatly typed pages lying on the pale rag rug, and one by one, tore each sheet in half, then in quarters, then in eighths. When she was finished she felt better, a little less frustrated. She got up again, tossed the paper into her wastebasket, and heaved a sigh. "What's the matter with me?" she wondered aloud.

All day long she had worked and reworked her copy for Monday's sample radio presentation of her show. It had sounded good on paper. Spoken aloud it limped. In fact, the one time she played the tape back, she had started yawning. It was that bad. In a panic she had phoned Sasha for help, only to find out that Sasha was away for the weekend visiting her boyfriend, Rob. Now Karen was wondering if she was beyond help. Until she had tried to write this copy for the broadcast, she had regarded herself as a good writer, with a snappy, lively style. Now she was beginning to doubt she was any kind of writer at all.

Karen wandered over to her bed and threw herself face down on the handwoven spread. Part of the problem was Brian. Until yesterday he had been background music — now he was like a stereo turned up full blast, tuning out every other thought in her head. She rolled over on her back and stared at the ceiling. She liked Brian. She was sure of that. Last night Karen had fallen asleep thinking of him; she woke up still hearing the smooth musical sound of his voice. She had probably been listening to him all night in her dreams. "All-night talk radio!" she muttered. "Brian Pierson is like talk radio. I can't tune him out."

She sat up and pounded the closest pillow. The problem wasn't liking Brian — the problem was what to do about it, and what to do about her show. Having Brian on her mind was keeping her mind off her work. Karen had never thought of herself as that kind of girl. She had always thought that when she fell in love, love wouldn't be the whole world. This spacy, hazy feeling inside did nothing for her prose style. Falling in love was going to keep her from giving her all to her show. The timing couldn't be worse.

She hugged the pillow to her chest. She didn't like the idea of falling in love with a rival, but that's exactly what Brian was. She was determined to give *What's News* every chance in the world to win the contest, and she knew Brian was just as determined. He acted smooth and cool, but she sensed he was as serious about new music as she was about the news. And yesterday, after she left the sub shop, she suddenly didn't trust him.

When she had walked in, he was already there rapping with Peter, probably trying to sell his show. He had an in with Peter she didn't, and suddenly she resented him for that. Karen knew she was being unfair. Before she had ever thought up *What's News*, before she had ever run into Brian, he had been Peter's friend. She just didn't like having the odds stacked against her. It was like running a one-legged race against an octopus. The thought of Brian as an octopus suddenly cracked Karen up. Well, no matter what the odds were, before the race was over, she was determined to give Brian some competition he'd never forget.

Karen closed her eyes and pictured a racetrack. She and Brian were running neck-and-neck to the finish, where they broke through a pink-ribboned tape. "A tie!" someone cried, and a band started playing, and the two of them jumped up and down, arm-in-arm, hugging each other. Then the picture got fuzzy. Karen hugged her pillow tighter and wondered exactly how hugging Brian would feel.

Wanda's deep musical voice interrupted Karen's daydream. "Karen, the phone! It's a guy!"

"Oooooh!" Karen moaned, and slid off her bed onto the floor. "Marty Leonard. Pleeeeeze leave me alone," she begged, and reached for the old-fashioned French-style phone on her night table.

She put the receiver to her ear. "Hi," she said dully.

"Karen?"

Karen sat up. Marty's voice was slow and soft with a kind of lazy drawl. This voice was bouncing and alive. . . . She grabbed her hair with one hand and bounced up and down a little on the floor. Then she cleared her throat and tried to sound sophisticated. "Who's this?" she asked.

"The *Soundings* man himself — Mr. Brian Pierson!" He paused a second, then asked brightly, *"What's news?"*

Karen groaned at his pun. "Oh, I don't know." She stood up and twiddled the cord on her phone. She glanced across the room into her mirror as she talked, surprised to see how happy she looked. "Karen, control yourself," she muttered with her hand over the receiver. Then she realized Brian had been talking about something nonstop for at least two minutes now. She pursed her lips and rolled her eyes to the ceiling. Talk

177

radio! she thought to herself. "Talk radio!" The words slipped out of her mouth before she realized it.

"Huh?" Brian said.

"Oh, nothing."

"Nothing?" Brian snorted into the phone. "I ask you if you want to go to Toons tonight to hear your sister's pal, Charlie Walker, play with that hot new trio, and you say, 'Talk radio!' I think you've been working too hard!"

Karen's mouth fell open. He had just asked her out on a date and she hadn't even heard him. And then she had said something unbelievably dumb. She sat down heavily on her bed and stared across the room. She dropped the receiver into her lap and tried to figure out what to do next. She barely knew this guy and already he was giving her a case of fried brains. Go out with him tonight? Karen was tempted. That fuzzy feeling she had inside as she thought of hugging him came back. But she couldn't go to Toons with him. It just seemed all wrong. Their date was going to have to wait until after the radio contest was over. Karen needed to keep a clear head until then and she had a lot of work to do by Monday. Seeing Brian wouldn't make things easier.

"Karen?" Brian's voice sounded very far away. Karen looked down. What was the receiver doing in her lap?

She swallowed hard and picked it up. "Talk Radio, you know, that hot new band," she improvised. "I wondered if they were going to be at Toons."

Brian suddenly sounded unsure and hesitant. "Talk Radio? Oh yeah — I know them." He slipped into his cool know-it-all tone of voice and Karen couldn't believe it. There was no band by that name and here he was faking that he knew all about them. "No, they don't play the jazz circuit," Brian went on smoothly. "I think they've played at the punkier joints, you know, like the Gladiatorium." He paused. "So, you wanna go tonight? Is it a date?"

"Uh, no, actually," Karen said, annoyed but also amused by his act. "I don't think I can make it tonight. Maybe some other time, in a couple of weeks, maybe?" She hoped she didn't sound too eager.

"Oh," he said.

"Well, I've got to go now."

"Uh, yeah." Brian's voice sounded flat and dull. Maybe she hadn't sounded eager enough. When he hung up, Karen held the receiver in her hand a second longer.

Suddenly, Wanda burst through the door. "Karen, what are you doing?" Karen was still sitting there, the phone in her hand, staring off into space.

She turned around guiltily and hung it up.

"Who was that?" her sister asked.

"Oh, a guy." Karen tried to sound noncommittal. She hadn't figured out yet why she had turned him down — she had just been daydreaming about him and wanted to be with him. What was the matter with her?

"I know it was a guy." Wanda tapped her foot impatiently, then studied her sister's face. She sat down beside her on the bed. "So it was *the* guy." Her voice softened.

Karen couldn't keep the smile off her face. "I guess — I mean, I don't know." She looked up at Wanda. Her sister had changed since she'd moved to New York. She looked older, more sophisticated, even more like the famous opera star she dreamed of becoming. She'd cut her hair very close to her head, playing up the striking beauty of her high, sculpted cheekbones and strong-featured face. Her gold hoop earrings were large and very dramatic. Wanda was slender and willowy like Karen, but she gave the impression of being larger than life. Karen could almost picture her in a gilded costume gliding across the Metropolitan Opera House stage performing *Tosca* or *Aida*. But she suddenly couldn't picture herself confiding in Wanda about Brian. She just didn't feel like talking about it right now. Besides, there wasn't really anything to tell. So she said, "Yeah, there's this guy. It's going okay."

"Are we still on for tonight?" Wanda had gotten up and was rifling through Karen's closet, holding one dress up after another and studying the effect in the mirror. Finally she selected a gold-knit dress that was very clingy and fashionably long. "Can I borrow this? Karen, what's wrong?" she cried as she turned toward her sister. Karen was staring at Wanda, her hand to her mouth, horrified.

Then she threw herself face down on her bed and wailed, *"Waaaada!* You won't believe what I've just done." Karen buried her face in her pillow and moaned miserably. Talking to Brian, just listening to his voice, she had forgotten all about her date with Wanda to go watch Charlie Walker at Toons.

Toons was a dark, smoky place that Karen had been to once before. It was one of the hottest jazz spots in the D.C. area and it drew a polite, knowledgeable, urban crowd — a mixture of young professionals, college kids, musicians, and important government officials out to give their distinguished foreign visitors a touch of real American culture. Karen knew it was a very important place for Charlie to be playing. He was only nineteen, but he was already sitting in with some of the big-name bands.

Karen hadn't been able to figure out a way to stay home. Wanda had made a big deal about the two of them going out together on one of her few weekends home from college. And Wanda had also reminded Karen that lots of her friends would be there expecting her. Karen listened to all of this as Wanda drove their mother's Mazda down to Georgetown, praying that Brian Pierson wouldn't be there, too.

When they walked in the lights were so dim, she had trouble seeing anything but the floodlit stage and a couple of front-row tables. Then the set was over, the lights came up, and Wanda waved at Phoebe, who was seated between Michael and Peter Lacey at a table in the middle of the room. Karen gave a weak wave, too. Seeing Peter unnerved her. There were several empty chairs at the table, and a couple had coats on them. Monica was probobly there, too, and. . . .

"Oh, no!" she moaned and considered bolting for the ladies' room. But it was too late — Brian had turned around, spotted Wanda, and then looked past Wanda right into Karen's eyes.

Karen wished the floor would open and swallow her up. She looked away quickly, but not before noticing a flash of disappointment in Brian's eyes. He looked hurt for just a second, before a wide grin crossed his face. Karen and Wanda joined the group.

By the second set Karen decided she had never been so miserable in her life. Everything was going wrong, *everything*. Once Brian had gotten over being hurt, he had slipped back into his smooth, glib act, hogging the conversation, at every turn bringing it back to the radio show, the contest, and the upcoming on-air sampler session. The longer she sat there listening to Brian, the more she wondered exactly what she had seen in him in the first place.

At first Peter had egged Brian on, delighted that he was taking the contest so seriously. Karen had kept her mouth shut. She was embarrassed and humiliated. Her sister had somehow figured out Brian was the boy who had called earlier in the evening and it was pretty obvious that Karen was the one person at the table he wasn't talking to now.

He was straddling his chair, fiddling with objects on the table. Karen's attention was divided between fascination in watching him stack nap-

kins, salt and pepper shakers, straws, and ash-
trays into a teetering tower ready to tumble any
second — and listening to him drone on about
how great his show was going to be. The more
he talked about his show, the more she felt he
was subtly putting *What's News* — and her —
down.

"You know, Peter, my man, I can't wait to
hear the response to *Soundings*." His tabletop
sculpture toppled down with a clatter. Brian
kept talking without missing a beat, and began
stacking the objects again. Then he leaned his
elbows on the small round table and peered intently at Wanda, who was sitting directly across
from him.

"Hey, Wanda, remember that tape you sent
me of the Harmonic Choir? I want your opinion," he said very earnestly, "of how that might
go over with the Kennedy crowd." Before Wanda
could say a word, he rattled on, "On the other
hand, 'Einstein on the Beach' — if I could figure
what two-minute segment to use — might go
over better. It's so hard knowing where to start.
New music is so *new* to most of the kids at
school, they don't even know what it is." He shot
a glance at Karen. "*Soundings* is going to open
up a whole new universe to them."

Karen pursed her lips, then sat up very straight
and said, "With you hosting *Soundings*, I'll be
surprised if anyone gets a chance to hear *any*
new music. By the time you stop talking, whatever's new about it is going to be ancient!"

Peter and Monica exchanged a worried glance,

but Michael and Wanda cracked up. Brian was stunned into silence, but only for a second. His eyes lit up as he met her challenge and he said in a cheerfully offhand way, "At least *Soundings* is new, different, creative. News at Kennedy travels best over the grapevine, so who needs the airwaves for *What's News*, anyway?" He gave her a sympathetic pat on the head.

Karen glared at him. Before she could think of a suitable jibe, Peter broke in, "Hey, you two, this is getting awfully boring, you know. I don't know about anyone else, but Monica and I would like the weekend off from WKND, and the contest, and the in-fighting. Neither of you have to convince me your shows are good. You've got to convince everyone else now. So keep the fireworks for Monday, high noon, in the broadcast booth. It'll be good, wholesome entertainment, I'm sure." Just then, to Peter's delight, Charlie walked over and pulled up a chair, and the conversation turned to music shop talk.

Karen sank down in her seat. Peter was right. She shouldn't have dug into Brian like that, but she couldn't help it. She couldn't help but feel he was carrying on so much about new music and *Soundings* not just to *im*press Peter, but to *de*press her as well, to get back at her for turning him down tonight. She couldn't blame him. Karen had said she couldn't go and then she had turned up at the very place he had invited her. In his shoes, she'd feel pretty crummy; she probably would have walked out immediately. In fact, that's what she'd do now. Charlie had finished a set and maybe Wanda was ready to leave. As Karen looked up, another group was about to start playing. If she wanted to get out, she had to get out now, before she disrupted the performance.

"Wanda." She tugged at her sister's sleeve. Wanda turned around, keeping one arm over Charlie's shoulder. "Can we go now? It's getting late, and Mom wouldn't want me out so — "

"Go?" Wanda eyed her sister incredulously. "Charlie's got two more sets. Mom won't mind if you're late tonight. She knows you're with me — you aren't going to get into trouble." Karen grimaced as Wanda cast a meaningful glance in Brian's direction.

Then Karen realized that Brian had suddenly fallen silent, too. Peter's speech must have had an effect on him.

He suddenly spoke up. "I can drive you home, Karen. It's getting stuffy in here, and whether Wanda's here or not, *I've* still got a curfew to stick to."

Wanda arched her eyebrows. Karen wanted to wipe that knowing smile off her sister's face. "It's up to you," Wanda said. "But I'm staying." She purposely turned back to Charlie, leaving Karen to make up her mind.

Drive home with Brian. At first the thought of driving home with Brian seemed preposterous, then scary, and finally right. She owed it to him, along with some kind of explanation about how she ended up here tonight, how she wasn't setting out to insult him or anything. Maybe she'd even tell him that if it weren't for the radio contest, she'd rather be with him than anyone.

Except for the whoosh of wind through the car window and the peculiar sounds issuing from Brian's tape deck, the ride home was silent. Karen sat primly on her side of the seat trying to think out the words to tell him what was going on between them — or at least what she thought was going on between them.

"So, do you like it?" His voice sounded relaxed, easy. He kept his eyes on the road as he spoke.

"Uh, what?" Karen asked. She noticed they were still only halfway to her house. He had taken the long way home and wasn't driving very fast. As they rolled down the main street of historic Rose Hill, they passed Sasha Jenkins' big house. Not seeing Sasha's Rabbit in the driveway made Karen's stomach feel funny. She needed her friends to talk to tonight.

Brian popped the tape out and clicked in another. This one grabbed Karen's attention. It was eerie, flutelike music. Maybe it *was* some kind of flute. The first tape had reminded Karen of some kind of squishy bug slithering across glass. These sounds reminded her of silk. "I like this one better," she said.

Brian arched his eyebrows and looked at her for the first time. "Good taste, this guy's a master. His name's Kitaro. The other one's by me."

"You made those noises?" Karen stared

straight into his eyes, amazed. "How?" she asked, afraid to hear the answer.

"On a synthesizer."

"You mean this stuff is music?"

"New music." They were stopped at a light. Brian looked into her eyes again. There wasn't the hint of a challenge in his face. He seemed eager for her to understand something.

Karen looked down at her hands. She was wearing dove-gray mittens that matched her coat. Mittens suddenly seemed so young, not at all right on someone who was almost seventeen. She pulled them off and stuffed them into her bag. Then she went back to trying to figure out what Brian wanted her to understand. But Karen found it hard to think. She wasn't sure if it was Brian or the silky music. It was doing something to her, taking away all her words.

When she looked up, they were climbing the steep hill approaching her house. "Here." She pointed toward the cul-de-sac at the end of the block. Her mother had left the porch lights on, and the light from the TV shone through the curtains of the family room. "I live here," she said.

Brian didn't pull into the circular driveway. He parked at the curb. It was dark in the car. Last week the street lamp had blown out. Karen's father had called the highway department three times, but no one had come to fix it yet.

Brian turned off the ignition but the tape kept running. Karen's hands were suddenly sweaty and her heart was racing. Here they were, parked in front of her house, right where her mother could look out the window and see them. Now Karen had to get out of the car and she hadn't yet told Brian she was sorry about tonight, and that she wanted to go out with him sometime . . . but not now.

When Brian reached across the seat and took her hand, she knew she didn't have to explain. "I know I come on strong, Karen. But — I like you." His voice didn't sound very strong. He sounded nervous and his hand trembled as he continued. "I kind of thought you liked me, too. Tonight — "

Instead of saying she was sorry, Karen put her finger to his lips. "Shh. You talk too much sometimes, like talk radio. Just listen." The music floated through the car and settled over them like a shawl. Then they were leaning toward each other across the seat. Karen steadied herself with one hand on the gearshift. Just before their lips met, they both hesitated. Karen's heart skipped a beat just before his lips met hers in a shy, gentle kiss.

He pulled back and played with the braids in her hair. She had wound lots of silver beads in them, like a picture she had found in a magazine. She had on one of her favorite dresses, and for once she knew she looked pretty. When Brian bent to kiss her again, he took off her glasses and whispered in her ear, "You're the most beautiful girl in the world!"

They kissed until the music stopped. The tape went on a second longer, then clicked off. Then something clicked on in Karen's brain. "Brian."

She pulled back a little. He looked up at her, dazed and very happy. She unwound her arms from around his neck and squiggled to a corner of the passenger seat. "Brian, I really like you." She fumbled on the dashboard for her glasses, When she put them back on it was easier to talk, easier to breathe.

"I can tell!" He smiled wickedly. He looked exactly the way he did when he used to launch his computer paper airplanes across Mayerwitz's study hall. Karen had a childish urge to tickle him. But if she tickled him, she knew they'd end up kissing again. Instead she fiddled in her bag and yanked out her mittens.

"But — "

He mugged a comic face. "But what? You've got a million other guys waiting out there? I don't care. I'll challenge them to duels — a war of words — "

"Will you shut up and let me finish!" she cried.

Brian pulled back slightly, a puzzled expression on his face.

"I like you and I want to see you again — "

"Do you think I'm going to give you any choice?" he quipped, but there was a tender catch in his voice that set Karen's heart singing.

"But not until after next Friday." There, she had said it.

"Why?" he asked bluntly, folding his arms across his chest.

"For the same reason I didn't want to go out with you tonight." Karen stopped Brian's protest with her hand. "Because I think it's wrong.

I mean we're competing for the same radio spot. That's a pretty big deal around school. People will talk — they'll think one of us might be letting the other one win. Stuff like that. You know how the grapevine is."

As soon as she said it she wanted to die. She hadn't mean to refer to Brian's jibe in Toons.

Brian frowned. "I'm not going to try to lose that spot because of you. *Soundings* versus *What's News* is one thing. You and me is another."

"But people will talk." Karen continued to press the point. The magical atmosphere in the car had vanished. She felt the tension building up again. She wanted to stop it before something got out of hand. She didn't want to destroy the incredible feeling between them, so she playfully tapped Brian's arm. "For all I know, you kissed me just now to get me to throw in my towel, to give up all thoughts of *What's News!*"

"WHAAATTT!" Brian roared. "Of all the nerve. I can't believe you'd think that." He slammed his hand against the steering wheel. The horn blew. Karen cringed. Brian continued to sputter. "Well, let me tell you something. It *never* would have occurred to me." Brian fumed helplessly, then switched on the ignition and turned on the headlights. "Do you know why I never thought of it?"

Karen felt the heat rise in her cheeks. "I haven't the faintest idea."

Brian searched frantically for an answer. She could almost see the wheels churning in his head. "Because I don't need to bother, that's why!

What's News isn't any kind of competition as far as I'm concerned. Now, if you were hosting *Cloaks and Jokes* it would be different," he ended with an arrogant sniff.

"You creep!" Karen cried, then threw open her door and jumped out of the car. She didn't care if her mother saw her now. She didn't even care if her voice carried down the block and to the next neighborhood. "Well, let me tell you," she said, "the first hot news item on my show is going to be about you, about what a poor loser you are. In fact, you aren't even a loser. You aren't good enough to be running in this race!"

She turned away and ran as fast as she could across the wide landscaped lawn up the pillared porch of the stately house, tears coursing down her face. Karen threw open the door and tore up the stairs. Her mother was standing in the hall. "Karen?" she said. Karen didn't answer. She ran right past her mother into her room, slamming the door behind her. She threw herself on the bed and began to sob. Karen had no idea what had happened with Brian just now, but she had a terrible feeling she had just ruined the first real romance of her life.

Chapter
16

The numbers flashed on the mammoth scoreboard as the judge announced them: 6.9; 7.5; 7.5; 8.0; 8.0; 7.5. Along with hundreds of other spectators in the Ocean City Boardwalk Sportsdome, Molly Ramirez cheered. For the moment she forgot her problems with Ted, the terrible decision she had to make, and the dull ache inside her that seemed worse today than it had last night when she left him standing in front of the Martial Arts Center. She jumped up and down and screamed like crazy for her friend Katie Crawford, who had just clinched second in the regional gymnastics competition. As she had predicted to Molly before the event, if a certain fourteen-year-old Olympic-bound phenomena, rumored to be the country's next Mary Lou Retton, hadn't been in the running, Katie might have come out first.

Molly's grin matched Katie's as the pretty red-headed gymnast ran out to take her bows. A minute later, she bounced back to the sidelines, grabbed her sweat shirt from the Kennedy High team coach, and landed at Molly's side. "I did it!" she cried as the girls hugged each other fiercely.

"I knew you would," Molly said. "*You* knew you would." She punched Katie's shoulder lightly.

"Listen, Coach Brockett's going to take the team out for a victory celebration. Want to come?"

Molly's face clouded slightly. She wasn't really in the mood for a party, but she had invited Katie to stay over at her aunt's house for the weekend. It wasn't fair to spoil her fun. "Sure. But can I meet you there later? I'll bring the car. That way we'll have a way back after the party's over."

Katie agreed and headed off to join her teammates on the bench. Molly made her way through the crowded viewing stands to find a soda machine before the boys' gymnastic competition started.

She dumped a handful of dimes into the vending machine and pressed one of the plastic buttons. Nothing came out. "Drat!" she muttered and yanked the coin release a couple of times. When that didn't work, she kicked the base of the machine. She kicked so hard her toe hurt. She hopped up and down a couple of times, then lost her balance. She fell backward against someone heading into the arena.

"Watch out!" he yelled. A strong hand grabbed her arm. She whirled around, ready to curse.

"Ted?" she nearly shouted. She stood there

holding her foot while he held on to her arm. A thought flashed across Molly's mind: He followed me. But then she noticed the shocked expression on his face matched her own. He hadn't expected to find her here.

He dropped her arm. "What are you doing here?" he asked.

"Katie Crawford's a friend of mine. I came to watch the meet. We're staying at my aunt's." Molly deliberately put a couple of paces between them.

Ted responded to the question she didn't ask. "Same here. I mean, I don't really know Katie, but I came to see a couple of buddies from Kennedy, too."

He looked away. Molly rubbed her foot gingerly. Neither of them spoke for a couple of minutes. It seemed ridiculous to just walk away from each other. Molly spoke up first. "Well, I'm going to watch the boys' meet myself. Should we — "

She was about to suggest that they sit together, but Ted interrupted. "I think I'll go outside. I can see the guys some other time."

Molly zipped up her Forty-Niners jacket and followed Ted out onto the boardwalk. The wind was icy and for a second she had trouble catching her breath. Ted walked on ahead of her.

The boardwalk was deserted. The ocean pounded the shore. Between the wind and the sound of the surf, the noise was deafening. The tide was in and higher than Molly remembered it ever being last August. In some places the waves lapped against the first couple of steps leading up to the boardwalk. Molly had the feeling they were the only two people in the world. Ted's scarlet varsity jacket stood out in bold relief against the gray weathered wood of the boardwalk, the dull water, and the bleak sky stretching out into a vague horizon. Except for the Sportsdome and the video arcade, all the other concessions were closed. Sheets of plywood were tacked over their gaudy exteriors. All the life she remembered from the summer was gone. Even Cheap Thrills, the small amusement park at the end of the boardwalk, was closed.

Ted stopped walking and leaned against the railing to look out to sea.

Molly positioned herself next to him. She wasn't sure what to say. There had been so much between them. The silence felt unnatural. She turned up her collar against the wind; Molly had never felt so cold in her life.

"I thought a lot about what happened yesterday," Ted said without looking at her. His voice was barely audible over the wind. His hands were clasped together so tightly his knuckles were white.

"Me, too," Molly admitted.

"I think you're right."

Molly drew her breath in sharply. It hurt to hear him say that. She had hoped somehow he could convince her she was wrong.

"We're both going to hurt a lot . . ." Ted continued. A small vein was pounding in his temple. ". . . when you go home again."

"That's why maybe it's better we don't start things up now," Molly said without conviction.

The wind seemed to swallow up her words.

Ted turned toward her. She didn't think he had heard what she said. Molly was sure he hadn't when she heard what he said next.

"I don't think it matters, Molly. We still love each other."

"I know that," she heard herself respond. She felt as if someone else were speaking. Molly sounded so calm, so in control. Her insides were doing somersaults, her hands were clenched in her pockets. It took all her strength not to touch Ted. "I just want you to give me a little time." She felt her resolve weakening.

Ted gazed at her, his blue eyes teary from the wind. "Okay," he said, but from the look on his face Molly could tell all the time in the world wouldn't change his feelings.

He took a deep breath and lolled his head to one side, working out a kink in his neck. "Well, what do we do now?"

Molly knew she should suggest going back to the Sportsdome, pretending they hadn't seen each other. Instead she said, "I don't know."

"Since we're here together — " Ted said as he took a step toward her.

Molly's body stiffened.

" — we could go hang out somewhere. You could tell me about the warm California weather." Ted's tone lightened and a smile appeared on his face. "Or you could tell me about life in Sausalito, what an East Coast bum who's never been there is missing."

Molly started to smile back. She couldn't help herself. Suddenly she had a feeling all her decisions were being made for her. She felt like someone who had almost drowned and then was rescued, but she didn't know if letting herself spend time with Ted was the rescuing part or the drowning. "Where could we go? It looks like everything's closed."

"The mall?"

"What about Katie?" Molly said. She couldn't take her eyes off Ted's. "I told her I'd meet her later, when the team's party breaks up."

"What time?" Ted didn't touch her, but his lips were only inches away from hers. The wind was so strong, Molly felt like it was pushing her right into his arms.

"After the last event. Five or so. I don't know." The damp salt air stung Molly's eyes. Her thick curls whipped across her forehead.

An incredibly joyous smile spread across Ted's face. "That gives us two whole hours." He made it sound like it was all the time in the world. He opened his arms wide. Molly held back only for a second, then abandoned herself to Ted's embrace, suddenly not caring about what came next for them.

"You know *Ted Mason*?" Katie exclaimed. "You were with him *all* afternoon?" She was sitting on Molly's cousin's bed in the second-floor bedroom of the small frame house. Molly's cousin Kara was away at college in Chapel Hill. Several magazines were spread out on the bed. Katie was plaiting her hair into a dozen braids.

Molly sat cross-legged on the floor and toyed with the hem of the extra-large San Francisco

Giants T-shirt she used as a nightgown. She had left Ted a few hours before outside the movie theater, then wandered around until she found Katie and the rest of the gymnastics team pigging out at Jumboland.

Downstairs, her aunt and uncle were already asleep. Molly tried to keep her voice low, but even whispering Ted's name out loud made her feel better. "We had this thing last summer," she began to explain. She went on to tell Katie the whole story. About the summer, about the fall, about going home, and missing Ted so much. About not being able to forget him. Somehow Molly managed not to cry, even when she told Katie about her decision not to call Ted when she got to Rose Hill. She told Katie how wonderful it had been when he found her last night and how confused she felt now.

Katie stopped braiding her hair. She propped her hands on her knees and regarded Molly intently. "I think you're crazy," she said firmly. "A guy like Ted Mason — I'd give anything to have someone love me the way he loves you. Anything."

Molly shook her head miserably. She wiped a tear from her cheek and stood up. She put her hands in the small of her back and leaned back and stretched. "I told him I'd let him know by Thursday what I thought we should do."

Katie rolled her eyes toward the ceiling. "All winter, nothing's changed — for either of you. And you expect something to be different by Thursday — give me a break."

Molly startled herself by laughing. It was the

first time she had laughed in weeks. She flopped down on the bed next to Katie and finished braiding the last section of her hair for her. "I know it doesn't make sense. But I can't stand feeling this way, so out of control. I've been in love before, but it never affected me this way. I wish Ted and I could just be friends."

"And I wish I were Mary Lou Retton."

Molly laughed again and tugged about six of Katie's braids, not very gently.

"OUCH!"

"Sshhhh!" Molly put a warning finger to her lips, then pointed down through the floor toward her aunt and uncle's room. She leaned back on her heels and held Katie's purple wide-toothed comb in her lap. "Actually, I don't wish we were just friends," she admitted in a small voice. "I just wish it didn't hurt so much."

Katie wheeled around and put her hands on Molly's shoulders. She gave her a little shake. "Molly, you act like you know exactly what's going to happen. You gave me this big speech the day we met about being free, living for the moment." Molly cringed hearing that. She had told Ted the same thing last summer. She believed it, too, in most circumstances. But in this case there was too much at stake to live for the moment.

"Your mother might actually get tenure at Georgetown, you know," Katie continued. "You might end up staying here."

"And I might not."

"That, too! But you've got to take a chance."

Molly got up and tossed the comb on the bed.

199

She padded over toward the dresser and looked past the pictures of Kara's prom and her old boyfriend and a sad yellowed snapshot of Samantha, Kara's golden retriever that had died last spring. She looked at her reflection. Her face was windburned and it stung. She put her hand to her lips, her neck, and remembered what it felt like to be kissed by Ted.

"I guess I'm more scared than Ted is," she finally said. She hadn't put her feelings into words until now, but they were strong feelings, and as she spoke her voice shook slightly. "I'm afraid of Ted's friends, too. You know, like Phoebe, and Chris, and the rest of that crowd. They're so, so — I don't know. Like the kids I used to make fun of at home. The most popular, the smartest, the most active. I've never felt right with people like that. And what will they think about me, you know, in comparison with Chris?"

Katie didn't answer right away. She tucked her comb in her bag and tossed the magazines off the bed. "I don't know what to say about that. I know a couple of kids in that crowd — Dee, Marc Harrison. They're really nice. I get the feeling they're not as exclusive as they look. I mean, Phoebe — "

Molly's shoulders tightened. "I'm not sure what I think about Phoebe."

Katie tossed a pillow in Molly's face. "Come off it. You should be glad she sent that dumb cookie. She only promised not to *tell* Ted and she kept her promise. Be fair."

Molly didn't feel like being fair, but she smiled. Katie was right. It wasn't a bad thing

Phoebe had done. In fact, it was just the kind of thing Molly might have done herself, wriggling around the truth a bit so someone wouldn't get hurt. Phoebe had known Ted a long time, and she was only trying to help him.

"And as for Chris," Katie said, "I don't think anyone would be comparing you two. Look, she's been going out with this new guy a few months already. If he can take comparison to Ted, then I think you can take it, too," Katie tried to joke.

"I know," Molly answered, unsure of herself. She hated feeling so insecure and she still didn't like the idea of being compared to such a paragon.

Katie flicked out the Snoopy lamp by the side of her bed and crawled under the covers. "What's important isn't what the crowd thinks or does. What matters is loving Ted."

Molly didn't answer. She sat for a long time at the dresser, staring into the mirror, thinking about what Katie had said. What really mattered was Ted and how much she loved him. Again Molly had the feeling her decision had finally been made for her.

Chapter
17

Bart shifted in his saddle and surveyed the rolling countryside below. In the middle of one of the meadows, Maryland ended and Virginia began. It was a sleepy Sunday landscape: white farmhouses, red barns, and miles of wooden fences. Acre upon acre of pastureland glittered gold and brown and rust in the noonday sun. In the distance, he could make out the hurdles and hedges of a steeplechase course at the start of Virginia horse country. The picture was beautiful and serene; so tamed and trimmed. It didn't match Bart's edgy, wild mood at all. Beneath him, the spirited stallion stirred restlessly, chafing at the bit. "Steady, Jagger," Bart soothed, patting the quivering black neck. "I know exactly how you feel."

All morning he had kept the horse to a safe walk or easy trot along the narrow ridge winding through the woods above Danberry Stable. Jagger hadn't had a good long workout in a couple of weeks, and Bart wanted to exercise him gently. Exercising the horses at the stables had become an occasional winter job for Bart and Diana. They had started out helping break the truckload of wild horses that landed at Danberry in the fall. Most of the animals, which had been rescued from almost certain doom at a slaughterhouse, had since been auctioned off to good homes. But Irene Danberry, who owned the stable with her husband Jack, had fallen in love with "Bart's horse," as the fiery stallion had first been called, and decided to keep him and give him a name. It was Holly who finally landed on the perfect one. The black stallion was like one of the wild horses from Mick Jagger's classic song. He had been Jagger ever since.

The horse snorted impatiently. Bart went a little further along the ridge toward a break in the trees, where a steep trail led down to a stream and into the open fields below. As he rode he thought of Holly, and how she should be with him now, sampling the first trail ride of early spring. He'd be on Jagger, she'd be on Galahad, a sweet-tempered bay gelding. They'd ridden these paths so many times together before winter had really set in. Riding Jagger without her along somehow seemed all wrong. It was his own fault she wasn't with him. He was the one who said he needed time to think. Bart gave a self-disgusted shake of his head. He took a deep breath, and gently prodded Jagger with his knees and let the reins go a bit slack. As the stallion carefully picked his way down the steep rocky slope and across the stream, Bart wondered if he was going nuts. He had given himself plenty of time to think, but he hadn't thought one bit about the problem he and Holly seemed to be having. He *had* thought of Holly though, all day and all night for three days straight, since he had seen her last. Bart couldn't stop thinking about her, and if he hadn't gotten into such a jealous fit over nothing, he wouldn't have to be thinking of her now. He'd be with her. "Einerson," he groaned, "if you lose that girl — " The thought was too awful to finish.

He suddenly kicked the horse hard. Jagger whinnied joyfully as Bart gave him his head. They galloped across the sun-drenched meadow, then through the next field and back again. The sun was warm, but there was a bite in the air, and Bart could almost imagine he was riding the range back home on his Appaloosa, Pete. Riding fast and free where there were no fences, no borders.

When he arrived back at the stable, Irene was standing on the back porch, a dish towel in her hands. The scent of Sunday dinner floated out across the barnyard. She looked approvingly at Bart and the horse. "Jagger needed that ride. Thanks, Bart. You have a way with him." She walked up and affectionately patted the stallion's neck. "It's late. Marnie can rub Jagger down. Just bring him over to the barn. You've done more than your share today." She started back to the house, then looked over her shoulder and said, "Want to stay for supper?"

Bart turned down the invitation. He wanted to get home. He wanted to call Holly. He jumped off the horse and led him to the barn. A girl approached and took the reins. "Marnie?" he asked. He hadn't seen her around Danberry before. He wondered if she was one of the new hands Irene had hired.

"That's me," she responded cheerfully. She lifted her big green eyes toward Bart but he didn't even notice her silky blonde hair, her skimpy shirt, her tight-fitting jeans. He left the barn and whistled all the way to his Jeep, thinking about Holly and how much he missed her . . . and loved her.

Sunday dinner was a Davis family tradition. Karen's father was a judge with an active political career and her mother headed one of Washington's largest social service agencies. The one time the family sat down together was Sunday, and nothing short of an earthquake could convince Karen's parents to let her skip the weekly ritual. Karen suffered through dinner the Sunday after her night out at Toons in silence. Wanda was home and Charlie had joined them, so no one seemed to notice that Karen didn't talk or eat a thing. She slumped down in her seat and shoveled her peas from one side of her plate to the other. Mechanically, she passed the butter, the rolls, the salt, all the while thinking what an absolute mess she had made of things with Brian, with the show, and with everything.

She didn't know what to do about it — last night her scene with Brian had seemed like the end of the world. But Karen wasn't the practical Davis sister for nothing. This morning she woke up knowing the world wasn't going to end just because she had had a fight with a guy she happened to like a whole lot. No, nothing so convenient as that. Tomorrow would dawn, just like today, but tomorrow she'd have to give her radio broadcast — and face Brian again. The thought was staggering.

If wanting to be with Brian had interfered with work on her show, being away from him had stopped it completely. She had moped around the house all morning, her head aching from tossing and turning all night. Wanda had cast a few sympathetic glances in her direction, but Karen pretended not to see them. She was embarrassed around Wanda and Charlie after the way she and Brian had behaved at Toons. She was just glad that neither of them had witnessed her argument with him in front of the house.

When the pie was neatly covered and the last dish was dry, Karen slipped up to her room and changed into her running clothes. Closing the back door behind her, she jogged across town to Dee's. She had already put out an s.o.s. on the phone and when she arrived, Dee was waiting, armed with tissues and a pot of tea.

"Fiona's here. She turned up a little while ago. Do you mind?" Dee asked as Karen hung her hat on a hook by the door. "At the sub shop last week, she figured out something was going on between you and Brian. So I filled her in a little just now." Dee sounded worried about betraying Karen's confidence.

"It doesn't matter, Dee," Karen assured her

with a sigh. "I need all the help I can get." She followed Dee down the hall to her bedroom.

Fiona sat cross-legged on the purple rug, sewing ribbons on her toe shoes. She looked up from the floor, her delicate face screwed up with concern. "Dee told me," she said, and patted the seat of a small easy chair nestled between a tall potted plant and the bed.

Karen sat down and told the girls her story. "I don't know what to do — everything is so messed up." A lone tear made its way down her cheek. "I've been so upset I haven't been able to work on my show and now I'm not prepared at all. I'm scared to death about the broadcast tomorrow. . . . Maybe I should just forget it." She buried her face in her arms.

Dee was by her side instantly. "Stop that, Karen. You're not going to give up on *What's News*. I won't let you — and Sasha won't either."

"Besides," Fiona added, "if you do quit, then it was all for nothing. You chaps fighting, and all last night. The whole point was you were afraid to start dating Brian because you thought it might jeopardize the outcome of the contest."

At the mention of Brian's name, another tear trickled out of the corner of Karen's eye. Dee smoothed her hand over Karen's back, not knowing what to say. She and Fiona exchanged a glance. Fiona stopped sewing. She tapped the toe of the pink satin shoe gently against the floor and stared thoughtfully at the ceiling. After a few minutes she spoke again. "Karen, you do really like him, don't you?" she asked gently.

Karen emitted a soft, "Yes."

"Then you have to let him know that. You have to clear the air."

Dee agreed with Fiona. "She's right, Karen." Karen looked up and met Dee's eyes. She sniffed noisily as Dee handed her a tissue.

"You mean apologize?" She didn't know if she was scared or horrified at the thought.

"Sort of. Just tell him you didn't mean to say the things you did. That you're confused — it never hurts to be honest."

"Confused?" A faint smile hovered around Karen's lips. "I'm so confused, I don't even know what I'm confused about!" she cried.

Fiona dismissed Karen's comment with a wave of her hand. "Well, I'd say it's perfectly obvious, Karen, and I'd be confused if I were you, too. It's hard to compete with people. We all have to do it, though, if there's something we really want to do, and someone else wants it just as badly. Competing with friends is tough. With a guy you like, it's got to be tougher as well as confusing."

"But Brian said it's two separate things: *What's News* versus *Soundings*, and me and him."

"In a way it is — or should be." Dee propped her face in her hands and frowned in concentration. "But that's easier said than done. It's not so easy being friendly enemies."

"But we aren't enemies and we aren't friends, either," Karen wailed, jumping up. She balled the tissues in her hand and tossed them into the metal wastebasket next to Dee's desk. "That's the whole problem. We hardly know each other now. We're just on the verge of starting something that could be really special, but the show keeps getting in the way of our feelings." Karen looked from Dee to Fiona helplessly.

Fiona took a deep breath. "So you like him that much."

"Yes."

"Then tell him so, and let everything else take care of itself. Let him know how much you care, and do your thing tomorrow anyway. Do your best."

"But I don't even know where to find Brian," Karen said. For a second she thought she was beginning to hear things. Even if she could find him she'd never have the nerve to tell him how she felt. Not after last night.

"That's easy!" Dee jumped up. She walked across the room and rummaged through the clutter on top of her white Formica drawing table. Finally she produced a thick phone book. Dee licked her index finger and began flipping through the pages. "Here it is," she cried triumphantly. "He even has his own phone number."

"You want me to call him?" Karen gasped, casting a petrified look at Dee's bright red phone.

"Either that or march over there. I'd prefer the phone, myself. Too much family around on Sunday. A phone call is more private," Fiona said.

Karen sat down heavily on Dee's bed. She ran her hands through her hair. She had never thought of calling Brian. She squeezed her eyes shut and tried to picture him on the other end of a phone.

"What will I say?" she asked in a small, frightened voice.

"That last night was a mistake — " Dee started.

"But just the fighting part of it," Fiona interrupted.

Dee stifled a giggle. "Right. And then let him take it from there."

"Okay. I won't even mention the contest or the show tomorrow," Karen said slowly, suddenly agreeing it was a good idea. Calling Brian was scary, but at least she was taking some kind of action.

Karen took a deep breath and picked up the receiver. The phone rang four times. Then a weird, wailing sound pierced Karen's ear, and she flinched. Then she heard a voice. It was Brian's:

"You have reached the outer limits, the edge of your reality. Before you descend down through the stratosphere, listen."

A barrage of weird noises, beeps, and scrapes followed. Then Brian's voice came on again. *"Please leave a message at the bong. BONG!"*

Karen sat stunned and waved the receiver in the air. "I don't believe it," she whispered. "I got an answering machine!"

Dee and Fiona gasped.

"I can't leave a message on a machine. I mean, how can I tell a machine I really like him and I'm sorry and everything?" Karen stared at the receiver. With a deep sigh she hung up the phone.

For a few minutes no one said a thing.

"You could write to Candy Hearts," Fiona suggested lamely. "Or send him one of Kim's cookies."

Karen balled up Dee's pillow and tossed it in Fiona's face.

Chapter
18

"Just relax and be yourself!" Monica Ford said, sitting Karen down in the oak swivel chair outside the broadcast booth of the WKND studio.

It was Monday afternoon, time for the new show sampler. Luck of the draw had put Brian first. He was already in the booth and the on-air light was on. His proposal for *Soundings* was coming in loud and clear over the studio sound system. Karen took a deep breath and tried to take her eyes off Brian and concentrate on Monica's advice. She needed all the advice she could get. She rubbed her palms against her cords, but one second later they were sweaty again. Karen was so nervous she thought she might faint.

After the fiasco with Brian's answering machine, Dee and Fiona drilled her on her show. Karen had thought she wouldn't be able to come up with a thing, but Dee had pulled out her typewriter and got Karen to talk casually and naturally about why she thought *What's News* was the best choice Kennedy students could make. As Karen talked, Dee typed, and Fiona played audience. It must have worked, because the copy in Karen's hand now sounded bright, alive, and convincing.

But as convincing as it sounded, Karen knew she'd never come over as strong and as sure of herself as Brian. She was trying *not* to listen to him, but just the optimistic sound of his voice was pretty enticing. It wouldn't be too bad hearing him over the WKND airwaves five days a week.

Monica caught her staring through the glass window between the broadcast booth and the studio. She stooped down and pulled Karen's sleeve. "Hey, come on. It's not as bad as you think. All those knobs and dials — they scared me to death at first, too, but now I'm as comfortable with them as Peter. Broadcasting's really a cinch. Besides, Peter will be in there with you working the controls. And if you get the show, one of us will help you along until you get the hang of it."

Karen smiled. It was true she was scared to death of all that, but she wasn't thinking about it just then. She'd still been thinking about the weird way Brian had looked at her earlier when she walked into the studio with Nicole and Josh to draw straws to see who would go first. It had been hot in the cramped anteroom and everyone was nervous. She had expected a hostile, challenging look from Brian, not the warm, understanding look he'd given her. She didn't understand it, but it thrilled her a little and scared her a lot.

Karen forced her attention back to Monica and began to digest the last-minute pointers. Then a lovely sound floated out of the loudspeakers. Monica stopped talking and looked up. Karen held her breath. It was the same silky music Brian had played in the car Saturday night. Kitaro. Karen remembered the name. She slowly turned back to the broadcast booth. Brian was looking straight at her. He held her glance for a second, then went back to the knobs and dials. Karen started breathing again. The other day, Brian said he was going to play samplings of Laurie Anderson and Philip Glass. She remembered that clearly. Maybe Brian had played them; Karen wasn't listening. She only heard him playing the music she would always think of as theirs.

After Brian came Josh, then Nicole. Karen was last. At first, she had hated the idea of being last. Now the extra time had given her a chance to calm down. By the time she settled in front of the microphone, her heart was still racing and she still felt as if she might faint, but at least Brian was gone. Peter had made him leave after his presentation, just as he did Josh and Nicole. Peter's introduction was short and sweet. Before Karen could think, he had signaled to her to take over the mike.

She cleared her throat, then grimaced. The mike picked up every sound. Clearing her throat was the first thing Monica had told her not to do. Karen swallowed hard and began reading her proposal. She started slowly, too slowly, she realized, to get through within her time-limit and still have space to give her *What's News* news. She fought a rising tide of panic. Then Karen remembered something Sasha had told her that morning. Just be yourself and talk into the mike as if you're talking to your friends. That's the way to sell it best. Karen remembered that, put aside her notes, and began ad-libbing. It was easy once she got started. Within seconds she was talking from the bottom of her heart, explaining why Kennedy students needed and deserved a campus news broadcast, why she was the person to give it. The more she talked, the easier her sales pitch became. Then she switched over to the news part. Karen picked up her copy and read with rapid-fire delivery: a fast-paced sports report about the baseball team, the season's first practice, and the big scoop that the Orioles' scout had been talking to Max Williamson, Kennedy's ace pitcher. She reported the hiring of a new psychology teacher, and the student protests over the firing of a popular swim team coach. "The best news, however, I've saved for last." Karen began her concluding remarks: "One week from today, WKND will begin broadcasting a new show in its expanded air-time slot. It's up to you to choose that show. *Unicorns and Flugelhorns, Cloaks and Jokes, Soundings,* or *What's News.* This is your chance, Cardinals, to decide exactly what *you* want to listen to. So get up here and vote. Ballot boxes are posted outside the studio. And a week from today, you'll hear the inside story about the race on *What's News,* because I, Karen Davis, have every intention of being the one who's back here." She finished with a flourish.

Peter applauded silently as Monica took over the microphone and began a shortened version of the noontime show. Karen was glowing even before she read the approval in Peter's eyes. In her heart, even if *What's News* didn't make it, Karen already felt like she had won something. In spite of Brian, the awful weekend, and all her fears and doubts, she had stuck to her guns. She had done it. Karen had made her first real broadcast. And even if she didn't get another chance to broadcast for years, she had taken the first step on the road to making her dream come true.

Chapter
19

Holly snapped each snap of her lab coat very carefully. She stuffed her bookbag into the white metal locker outside the chemistry lab, and taking a deep breath, walked into the classroom.

Diana was already at their table with the day's experiment half set up. Her blonde head was bent over the lab book, and she was gnawing the eraser end of a pencil. When Holly approached, she glanced up and nodded coolly. She didn't smile, she just looked distant and embarrassed.

So nothing's changed, Holly thought miserably. She wanted whatever tension there was between them to be over. But she didn't know what to do, so she gave a short nod back, and started rearranging the beakers on the stone-top lab table. As usual, Diana had set things up all wrong. But today, instead of teasing Diana about being hopeless at chemistry, Holly worked in silence. She had hoped that over the weekend the air would have cleared between them. Since Thursday, they had barely talked at all. Holly still felt hurt, let down, and abandoned after their last conversation, but she hadn't phoned Diana to try to talk it out, friend to friend. In fact, she had avoided her until now. Today Holly had been looking forward to seeing Diana — she finally felt ready to talk and make things right again, between them — and between her and Bart, her and Matt.

Holly's hand shook slightly. The fragile glass beakers knocked together dangerously. "Watch out!" Diana cried. Holly put them down again, carefully. She wasn't in the best state of mind to be in a chemistry lab. She might accidentally cause some minor disaster. Suddenly she felt like she had to get out of there. She looked at Diana with pleading eyes. A flicker of concern crossed Diana's face.

Holly's bottom lip quivered. "Di, I need to talk. Everything's crazy." Her voice trembled. "I really need your help now." A tear started down her face. Holly ran out of the lab and into the bathroom. Pushing past a startled Ms. Barish, Diana followed instantly.

"What happened?" Diana cried, hurrying to Holly's side. She had never seen Holly like this: circles under her eyes, her face pale. She looked terrible. Holly turned her face away and pressed her cheek to the cold tile wall. Her shoulders shook with sobs.

Holly wanted to tell Diana everything, but she couldn't catch her breath enough to talk. Diana forced her to turn around. She threw her arms around Holly and whispered, "Hey, I'm sorry.

I'm so sorry for the other day. Is that what's wrong?"

Holly clung to Diana for a long time, burying her face in her friend's silky hair until her tears began to subside. She nodded yes, then no.

Diana was puzzled. She gnawed her lip thoughtfully. "Bart told me he was going to call you last night. I thought things were better."

Holly stared uncomprehendingly at Diana. "He-he called?" she stammered, wiping her cheeks with the back of her hand. Diana pulled some paper towels out of the dispenser. Holly dabbed at her eyes.

"You weren't home?"

Holly shook her head. "No. I was out with my mother and Bruce, looking at places near Maryville for the wedding reception. We stayed there for dinner, and I didn't get home until late. . . ." Her voice trailed off. Bart had called. "You think everything is okay again?" she whispered.

Diana nodded.

Holly slid her back down the wall and sat on the floor, drawing her knees to her chest. Her head was throbbing; her heart pounding. She was too numb to react. Bart had phoned, so seeing him now wouldn't be such a bad thing. A huge weight seemed to lift from her shoulders. Then she remembered Matt. She moaned softly and turned her face back to the wall.

Diana sat down beside her. "Do you feel better now — knowing about Bart?"

"Sort of." When she faced Diana, her eyes were full of pain. Diana put her hand on Holly's shoulder.

"What happened?" she said. This time her voice was very gentle and encouraging. Holly knew Diana wouldn't turn away from her now, no matter what she told her. They hadn't talked about their problems with their friendship, but all that was gone now. Holly confided, "Remember that guy, Matt?"

Diana nodded.

"Well, on Friday I ran into him on the bus to the planetarium." Holly found that she couldn't continue. Matt's intense dark eyes flashed in front of her. She didn't want to have to hurt him. She buried her face in her arms again, and started crying softly.

"Whew!" Diana suddenly comprehended. "Something happened between you." She sounded surprised, but not shocked, not critical.

"I didn't meant it, I didn't mean for anything to happen," Holly cried in despair. "He's just so nice, and I needed someone to talk to so badly, and one thing led to another. I was lonely." Her voice sank to a whisper again. "Oh Di, now I'm really going to hurt him. Matt Jacobs doesn't deserve that — he's such a sweet person."

"Don't tell Bart!" Diana's advice caught her off guard.

Holly hadn't even let herself think that far ahead. Her plan was to talk to Matt first, then Bart. Telling Bart she loved him was the important thing.

"How can I not?" Holly asked. "I can't lie to him."

Diana put a warning hand on Holly's shoulder.

"Wait then. Just until everything else between you is straightened out."

"I'm going to talk to Matt today, when school's out. I told him Friday it was wrong. But I don't think he wanted to hear me," she confessed. "I don't love him, Di. I'm still so in love with Bart."

Before Diana could respond, the door burst open. "Hey, you two. Aren't you supposed to be in Barish's chem lab?" Kim Barrie asked. She dumped her books on the sink.

Holly quickly splashed water on her puffy red eyes.

"Bio lab was canceled today," Kim said. "Someone let the frogs go again."

Diana laughed. "Sasha Jenkins' handiwork, I bet."

"No, she wouldn't do that — but she will praise whoever did in this week's editorial."

Kim began pulling a comb through her short, straight hair. She made a comical face into the mirror. "I am turning into the worst businesswoman in the world."

She grabbed her bag and began rummaging through it, finally producing two small boxes. "I was going to give these to Woody to deliver. But Ms. Daniels, since we've run into each other like this, I'll give them to you myself." With that she waved good-bye and hurried off.

"*Two* valentines?" Diana smiled until she looked at Holly's face.

"I guess one is from Bart," Holly said slowly, not saying a word about the other one. She opened the smaller pink box. The cookie inside said simply, BE MINE. Her hand shook as she unfolded the note. It was handwritten, in pencil. Before she even read it she smiled. She'd know the big scrawly writing anywhere. *I'm sorry. I really love you and I can't wait to see you again. I've missed you these past few days. Meet me after school on the steps by the courts. Bart.*

She stuffed the other box in her bag. Opening it, reading whatever was inside, would make things worse right now. "Di, I'd better go and find Matt. I'll have to make up the lab another time."

"I'll call you later!" Diana called out as Holly went running out the door. In minutes she was across the quad, a set expression on her face. All day she had let herself believe she had no idea where Matt was. Now she headed directly for the school shop.

Holly squared her shoulders and shoved open the swinging metal doors. She'd never been in the shop before. The clean dry scent of sawdust filled the air. Hand tools gleamed in neat rows by the wall and the long workbenches were clean. The place seemed deserted.

Holly held her breath. If Matt wasn't here, she didn't know what she'd do. She walked forward slowly, trailing her fingers along the smooth edge of the workbench. She gave one final look around, then started for the door.

"Hello?" a deep voice called. A figure emerged from the shadows along the opposite wall.

"Matt?" Holly said.

"Holly? What are you doing here?" He was across the floor in two or three steps. Then his arms were around her. Holly stiffened. Matt stepped back. He stared at her uncomprehendingly.

"You got my valentine?"

"Yes — yes, thank you," she said, deciding not to tell him she hadn't opened it yet. Giving it back to him seemed cruel. She put a couple of steps between them. She had no idea how to begin. She only knew she had to talk to him, to tell him the truth about her and Bart, and that she didn't love him.

Matt leaned against the table across from her. He crossed his arms and seemed to hold his breath.

"Matt, I tried to tell you Friday. It-it was a mistake." Holly hated the sound of her voice when she heard herself. She sounded harsh and uncaring, but she was afraid to stop and try again. Holly walked over to the wall and ran her finger along the smooth wooden handle of a hammer.

"Holly?" The catch in his voice made her turn around and face him.

"Oh, Matt," she cried. "I didn't mean for that to happen between us. It was wrong of me. I love Bart — I really do."

Matt's face clouded over. With the tip of his boot, he kicked a chunk of wood across the linoleum.

There was a terrible moment of silence between them. Holly had never hurt anyone like this before. And hurting Matt — he was such an incredible guy — seemed like such an awful thing to do. He had been so kind to her, so caring. One day some girl would fall in love with him, and

223

she'd be very lucky, Holly thought.

She started toward the door. There was nothing more for her to say. As she passed Matt, she stopped and looked up into his face. "Oh, Matt. You are such an incredible person." She threw her arms around him and hugged him tightly. He hugged her back so hard she thought she'd break in half.

After a moment he stepped aside. He followed her to the door, not touching her again. Holly turned around, one foot in the hall, one foot in the shop. "Matt, I meant that. I really do think you're wonderful. And I hope, someday, we can be friends," she whispered. Her hand rested briefly on his arm. She turned away and hurried off, her head down. Seeing Matt so sad made her heart ache. But in a few minutes she'd be in Bart's arms again, and as she turned the corner of the corridor, her step grew lighter and her heart did little flip-flops in her chest.

Bart galomphed down the back stairs and into the hall leading toward Kennedy's sprawling new west wing. A group of girls burst out of the visiting team locker room across from the gym. They were wearing blue basketball shorts; ST. MARY'S FLYERS and a blue-winged logo were printed on their tank tops. Bart maneuvered his way around them. One of the girls let out a low, sexy whistle and the others laughed. Bart was oblivious. He was remembering how Holly's hazel eyes were sometimes green like the color of the meadows behind Danberry Stable.

As he neared the shop he was inspired. He

hadn't exactly figured out what would happen when he saw Holly now, but he would tell her he loved her. And he wanted to do something very special to celebrate their reunion. He would take her out to Danberry. It had been so beautiful there. Yesterday Bart had noticed a tinge of green in the willows overhanging the creek. Picturing Holly's joyous look when she saw the first sign of spring, he smiled. A short afternoon ride up in the hills would be perfect. Bart glanced at the clock and quickened his pace; he didn't want to be late. But as he started around the corner, the smile on his face vanished.

Matt Jacobs was standing in the door of the shop. Holly was standing with him, her back to Bart. She was talking, but her voice was so low Bart couldn't hear what she was saying. He didn't have to, though. One look at Jacobs' face and Bart saw all he needed to. Matt Jacobs was in love. Holly touched Matt's arm lightly, then walked away. Bart reeled back a couple of steps.

For a second he didn't move. A wave of anger washed over him, then passed. Bart leaned back against the cold concrete wall and tried to get his bearings. Holly had told him there was nothing between her and Matt. They hardly knew each other, she had said, and yesterday he had finally had enough sense to believe her. But she hadn't been home last night when he called. Between Wednesday afternoon and now something must have happened. He looked over toward the shop. The door was closed again.

A week ago he might have walked up and punched Matt out. But now Bart's shoulders sagged, and he started back up the hall. He had practically thrown Holly into Matt's arms. Matt must have called her over the weekend. Whatever had happened, it was Bart's own fault.

The hall was deserted and silent except for the thump of a basketball and occasional screams and shouts from the girls' game in the gym. Outside the boys' locker room, Bart stopped. All he wanted was to scream and shout and tear into something, someone, anything. But the person he really wanted to strangle was himself. Bart balled up his fist and punched the wall, hard. Once. Twice. Three times. He felt like his heart was breaking. Holly just didn't love him anymore. He hard to learn to live with that fact. He leaned against the wall, propping his forehead against his arm. If only he hadn't gotten so jealous, none of this would have happened. Everything seemed so unfair. One mistake — one lousy mistake and he had totally blown his chances at being the happiest guy in the world.

Bart looked back down the hall. Holly must have been on her way to meet him, anyway, probably to tell him it was over. Bart knew he should turn around, go outside, and get it over with. She'd be waiting on the steps leading down to the tennis courts. He was already late. Holly would wait awhile longer — she was like that. Picturing her sitting there, the wind ruffling her soft hair, Bart let out a low moan. He couldn't face her now. He wouldn't be able to talk, anyway. His throat felt unbearably tight, his fist ached, and he felt a funny pressure building behind his eyes. He hadn't felt like this in ages.

* * *

For as long as she could, Holly pretended not to notice the shadows lengthening across the white concrete walk at the base of the steps.

When she had first left Matt and hurried down the hall and out into the sunlight, she had been disappointed Bart wasn't already there waiting. Of course, she *was* early. She sat down to wait for him. Then she was glad he wasn't there yet. Her mind was still muddled from the scene with Matt and it gave her a chance to clear her head. She gathered her thoughts and felt at peace with herself and very happy. Any moment now, Bart would come, and he would fold her into his arms and their troubles would melt away.

At three-thirty Holly checked her watch for a third time. Bart was never late for anything. Her stomach tightened. Her mind began reviewing all the things Bart might have done after his last class: something with the football coach, something to do with the Kennedy Players — Bart had said Woody wanted to tape him singing cowboy songs for a spot on WKND advertising forthcoming auditions for a spring production. The door to the hall was half open and noise from the gym drifted out toward her. Each time footsteps neared, Holly tensed up. Then they'd fade away and she'd get a sinking feeling in her heart.

By four, Holly knew she should leave, but she was almost afraid to get up, as if getting up and starting for her car would make the awful truth too real. Bart had stood her up. Why would he do this now, after that note — the valentine? An angry flush rose up her neck and onto her face.

She hadn't done anything to deserve being treated like this. It wasn't fair.

A high-pitched giggle followed by a lower laugh floated over from the tennis courts. Then the wire gate squeaked shut. Brenda and Chris Austin had finished their game. Holly jumped up. She didn't want them to find her here. An hour ago when they walked out of the locker room, she had said she was waiting for Bart. Holly didn't want to face her friends. They'd know Bart had stood her up.

Holly tied her sweater around her neck and hurried down the path toward the front of the quad. Then she broke into a run. Climbing into her Malibu and heading across the half-empty lot, she didn't even bother to check for Bart's Jeep in its usual spot. Holly pulled out into the rush-hour traffic creeping down Rosemont with just one thought on her mind: It was over. Bart and Holly were a thing of the past. There was no question about that now. She'd never know exactly why, and at the moment she didn't care. Holly was too angry and hurt inside. She only knew it was over, and if she thought about it too much she wasn't quite sure how she'd get through the rest of the day, or the night, or the week, or the school year.

Instead of driving home, she headed toward the west side of town and Rose Hill's medical clinic. Dr. Ellerbee was short on staff this week. He hadn't asked her to come in today, but he had said if she had any time, he could use a helping hand. At the clinic, helping people, Holly could keep her mind off Bart.

Chapter
20

Molly lugged the practice mats across the floor and began transforming the gymnasium into an akido dojo. It was Wednesday afternoon, time for her demonstration and talk on martial arts and self-defense for women. At any other time, in any other circumstances, Molly would have jumped at the chance to talk at length about akido. Right now, she dreaded it. There had been no way to gracefully convince Ms. Molinari that the after-school voluntary session should be put off. Even so, Molly wasn't sure there would *ever* be a good time. She hated the idea of being on display in front of all of Ted's friends.

The door squeaked open. Molly looked over her shoulder. Phoebe Hall stood in the entranceway looking a little washed-out in her regulation gymsuit. She hesitated, then heaved a deep breath and resolutely marched over to Molly.

Molly didn't know what to do. She dropped

down on her knees and continued laying down the mats. To her surprise, Phoebe began to help her.

For a few moments the only sound in the gym was the soft whoosh and thump of mats being dragged from the sidelines, then unfolded on the floor.

Phoebe finally sat back on her heels. "Molly," she began, her musical voice bouncing off the walls. "I'm sorry about Friday. About Ted and the valentine. I broke my promise. I've never broken a promise to a friend before and I feel crummy. I just wanted you to know." She said it all in just one breath. At the end, her shoulders sagged with relief. Phoebe folded her hands in her lap and sat very still waiting for Molly to say something.

Molly fingered the border of her loose white practice shirt and considered Phoebe's words carefully. She seemed so sensitive, so vulnerable, and very concerned. Molly realized she had never met anyone quite like Phoebe before. She could be so bubbly. Molly knew then that was why she liked her, why she had had a good feeling about her the minute she saw her last week in the akido studio. She also realized Phoebe had called her a friend just now. Molly smiled. "Forget it, Phoebe. It's okay. I was a little ticked off at first," she admitted, "but I think I would have done the same thing myself, so I guess it's okay. I can't really blame you. And now I don't have to hide from Ted or anyone else." A few wispy curls were stuck to her temples, and Molly shoved them back from her face. "I don't think you hurt anything, though nothing's solved yet between me and Ted."

Phoebe absentmindedly fingered the piping along the edge of the mat. She looked up thoughtfully at Molly. Just when she seemed about to say something, the gym doors burst open and the rest of the girls walked in. Molly's heart sank; the first one through the door was Chris Austin.

Phoebe looked around quickly and scrambled to her feet, tugging down the shorts of her gymsuit. "Don't worry, it'll be all right," she assured Molly. She scampered over to join the other girls.

As the girls lined up and Ms. Molinari introduced Molly, she felt her nervousness coming back. Chris was in the first row, and their eyes met for a second. Molly looked away. She forced herself not to clench her fist, to relax. In spite of Phoebe's optimistic predictions, the class would go just as Molly had expected. The kids who knew Ted, like Chris, had come to check her out, and she felt embarrassed, on display, and annoyed.

Molly had studied akido for six years now, so she wasn't surprised that the first twenty minutes flew by. She explained the principle of martial arts, the idea of *ch'i*, the life force flowing through the universe in all living beings. She felt herself calming down. By the end of the talk, she had almost forgotten about Chris and her fears about what the other kids were thinking.

When she finished talking, she asked for a volunteer to give a demonstration. Chris walked right up. "I'd like to try," she said, eyeing the black mat anxiously.

Molly caught her breath. She wondered if Chris was up to something, trying to prove something. Molly pushed her hair out of her eyes and met Chris's challenge coolly. In a second she sized Chris up: tall, muscular, athletic. Molly guided Chris to the center of the mat and said, "You won't get hurt, so don't be afraid. This move will show you how you can defeat your opponent, not by resisting her moves, but by flowing with them." She invited Chris to try and knock her over. Chris hesitated, then lunged toward Molly. Before Chris knew what hit her, she was thrown to the ground. She looked around startled, then glanced up at Molly, a look of admiration in her eyes. Molly reached down and helped Chris to her feet.

"How did you do that?" Chris exclaimed, dusting off her clothes. Molly tried to explain the move and with other volunteers, she demonstrated the move again and again.

Gradually, everyone began to catch on. At the end of the class, Chris stood up and announced, "I don't know about anyone else here, but I'm impressed. I think a lot of girls at Kennedy would be interested in learning these akido techniques. What does everyone think of forming a Martial Arts Club?"

The girls all cheered. Molly flushed with pleasure.

"Would you like to head it?" Chris turned to Molly.

"Are you kidding?" Molly whooped.

"The next student council meeting's on Monday at three. Why don't you plan to be there and

232

I'll introduce you to Jonathan Preston — he's the student activities director. He'll have some good ideas on how to get a club started."

The class broke up and everyone headed for the locker room. Molly stayed behind, gathering up the mats and trying to figure out exactly what had just happened. Chris Austin hadn't seemed jealous of her at all. Nothing like that, just a little curious. Molly giggled to herself. Who could blame her? She was curious about Chris, too.

A hand landed softly on her shoulder. Molly jumped and wheeled around. Chris was behind her, already dressed in trim beige pants, a tailored shirt, and a blue sweat shirt tied around her neck by its sleeves. She looked directly into Molly's eyes and said, "I know about last summer, about you and Ted. I hope things work out between you now. He's really missed you a lot." That was all she said, but to Molly, Chris's words spoke worlds. She couldn't believe this beautiful golden girl was so generous and forgiving.

Before Molly had a chance to respond, Chris went on. "Listen, Phoebe and I will clear this stuff up. Why don't you change, and come with us to Mario's. They've got the best pizza in town." Just then Phoebe walked up, snapping the straps of her overalls.

Molly hesitated only an instant. She looked over at Phoebe and grinned shyly. She gave her stomach an exaggerated pat and sank into a mock faint against the wall. "Sounds great. I'm starved," she said. Not just for food, she thought, but for company.

233

Jogging off to the locker room, Molly felt happier than she had in months. Her fears about Ted's friends had really been unfounded, just like Katie had predicted. Things might actually work out for her in this new school — once she figured out what to do about Ted.

Chapter
21

WKND's Valentine's Day Dance was two days off and Karen had decided she didn't need a new dress. After all, she didn't have a date, so what she wore wasn't *that* important. That's what she had told Dee and Fiona that afternoon when the three of them had gone shopping in Georgetown.

They had landed at Karen's house for dinner and now Dee was in front of the full-length mirror trying to decide if her pink dress was too long or too short. Dee swirled around once and looked for some advice from Fiona and Karen. "Maybe I shouldn't have bought this. Don't you think it makes me look a little fat?"

"Uggggh!" Fiona groaned. "Dee, it looks great. We both told you that a hundred times before you bought it. It could be a bit shorter, but if you wear heels it won't matter."

"So I shouldn't shorten it?" Dee looked worried, and craned her neck over her shoulder trying to get a glimpse of the back.

"Dee, just leave it alone. It's perfect," Karen pointed out. The flowing dress had a snug bodice and a very full skirt nipped in tight at the waist. Karen eyed it dreamily — she had always wanted a dress like that. She sighed audibly, then forced herself to stop being envious. She'd look absolutely ridiculous in something like that. It suited Dee perfectly, but Karen didn't have the right kind of figure for it, and she'd be swallowed up in the yards of skirt.

She marched over to the small gold box lying open on her bed and pulled out Fiona's outfit. "I still don't get how this one goes. Try it on again." She handed Fiona what looked like a tiny piece of metallic fabric.

Fiona giggled. She pulled off her top, and squirmed out of her miniskirt. Then she took the dress and pulled it over her head. She emerged looking all legs, very little dress, and more like a British rock star than a ballerina. She did a perfect pirouette in front of the mirror and kicked off her loafers. "Well, what do you think?"

Dee and Karen looked at each other, then imitating Fiona's British accent, exclaimed together, "SMASHING!"

Fiona covered her ears and groaned. A second later she threw open the door to Karen's closet. "But enough of us. You're the one who wouldn't buy anything. Now what do you intend to wear?"

Karen raised her eyes to the ceiling. "Like I told you guys, it's not important."

"Yeah, yeah, we've heard all about it," Dee said, and systematically began sifting through Karen's clothes. From the depths of the closet, she commented, "The WKND contest winner is going to be announced, and there's always the chance you'll be the winner. Then you'll have to get up on the stage in front of *everyone*."

Just then, the doorbell rang. Karen's parents were out, so she hurried downstairs and peeked through the glass panel of the front door. "Woody, what are you doing here?" She threw open the door. Woody rocked back and forth on his heels, grinning from ear to ear. He was wearing red suspenders dotted with tiny white hearts. "Sweets to the Sweet!" he said. He popped a large heart-shaped box right into Karen's hands and gave her a kiss. Brian, she thought. It must be from Brian.

"So who's it from?" Woody asked cheerily.

"Uh — I don't know," Karen lied. She managed to smile at Woody and shake a finger in his face. "I thought you were the one person at Kennedy High who Kim told *all* her secrets to."

Woody guffawed. "Nope. I mean, I know most of what the cookies say, but I missed out on this one. Kim didn't tell me." When he saw Karen's skeptical look, he crossed his heart. "Honest!" He waited a second to see if Karen would inform him, then shrugged sheepishly. "I get the message — it's none of my business." He slapped his forehead and groaned, "Well, it's time for me to get back to what *is* my business before Sweets to the Sweet gets way behind schedule." Imitating the White Rabbit checking his pocket watch,

237

Woody waved his hands frantically in the air and scampered down the circular drive to his cherry red Volvo.

Karen thought about hiding the box in the kitchen. She was sure — almost sure — it was from Brian. She turned around to walk back in, and bumped right into her two friends.

Dee's mouth fell open. "I don't believe it."

"Brian?" Fiona asked.

Karen gulped. "I think so." She stood there awkwardly, holding the box.

"Well, open it!" Dee insisted, dragging Karen back upstairs to her room.

Karen knelt on her bed and slowly undid the ribbon. She took a deep breath and opened the box. Inside was a large sugar cookie decorated with a single musical note.

She hadn't seen Brian since the broadcast Monday and they hadn't talked since their argument Saturday night. She thought about the funny look he had given her in the studio and about how he had seemed to play Kitaro just for her. But he hadn't made any attempt to get in touch with her since Monday. In the past couple of days she had decided she had imagined all that. Playing Kitaro was just a coincidence; the look was something that hadn't really happened at all.

But it must have — the cookie in her hand proved it. What had changed his mind since their argument the other night? Why did he like her again? Karen couldn't keep the smile off her lips. She suddenly flopped over on her stomach and buried her head in her pillow. Her voice came out muffled as she said, "He likes me. . . . I think he really likes me." Then she sat up and looked from Dee to Fiona and back to Dee. "I don't understand it, but he must. He does!" Her eyes were shining as she hugged her pillow to her chest.

Late that night, Karen crept out of bed and tiptoed into Wanda's room. She closed the door, then flicked on the light. Most of what made Wanda's room Wanda's was gone: the poster of a famous opera house in Italy that once hung over the bed; the autographed glossy picture of the great soprano, Leontyne Price, that used to sit on the desk; the giant stuffed moose she had won when she was three for singing "The Star-Spangled Banner" better than kids twice her age. But Karen barely noticed all that. She padded to Wanda's closet and peered inside. Except for a couple of blouses and a garment bag in the back, it was bare. Karen unzipped the bag very carefully and pulled out Wanda's concert dresses one by one.

She suddenly gasped in delight, and clapped her hand over her mouth. She bit her lip and looked around, but she knew her parents were asleep and hadn't heard her.

Two minutes later she was out of her nightgown and parading in front of Wanda's mirror. The dress was perfect. It was a narrow, clingy dress that ended just below the knee and had only one long close-fitting sleeve. It had always been a bit tight on Wanda, but it fit Karen per-

fectly. The silvery fabric was soft and shiny, and
the threads running through it sparkled when they
caught the light. Karen clasped her hands and
smiled. It was just the thing for Friday night; for
Brian.

Chapter
22

"Webster, you've finally out-Webstered yourself!" Marc Harrison shouted with glee.

It was Thursday afternoon, and the boys' locker room was packed. Not just with boys from last-period gym class, but with boxes. Gold boxes from Sweets to the Sweet. Woody had just made a frantic entrance on roller skates and sailed head-on into Bart Einerson. Woody's skates flew out from under him and the stack of boxes scattered across the floor.

Everyone had burst out laughing but Bart. He had stormed off to a corner and scowled. Woody sat dazed in the middle of the mess and grinned foolishly. "We promised you delivery. We didn't promise you delivery in one piece. Let's see, now." He picked up his right hand with his left and studied it. Then held his foot up toward his nose. He patted his black skate affectionately, and accepting Marc's hand, scrambled to his feet.

"Actually — " He made a big business of dusting himself off. "Nothing necessary seems to be broken — just a few hearts!" Woody shook one of the cookie boxes and it rattled as if it contained dozens of crumbled pieces.

"Speaking of broken hearts," Jonathan piped up, "exactly who do these belong to?"

Woody rolled his eyes. "Do you have to ask. . . ?" He looked around for Bart. The tall linebacker was nowhere in sight. "Mostly Einerson. But here's one," Woody reached into the pile and miraculously scooped up a big red box, "for Mason!"

Ted's hand instantly shot out. "Thanks, Woody," Ted said. With his towel still around his neck he ducked around the corner and headed for his locker.

Today was the day Molly had promised her answer. No one else would send him a valentine. Ted was pretty sure of that. He looked at the box in his hand and smiled. If Molly's answer was no, she'd never send a Sweets to the Sweet. Ted began laughing. A hearty, happy laugh, like he hadn't laughed in months. "Molly Ramirez, where are you?" he said to no one in particular. Without grabbing his books or his jacket he headed into the hall to find her, the valentine box tucked under his arm.

He spotted her instantly. She was sitting at the far end of the hall, scrunched against the soda machine, waiting for him.

A second later she was in his arms. He nestled his face in the soft skin of her neck and laughed again. Without saying a word, he scooped her off the floor and carried her to a private spot near the back stairs. Molly plopped down happily into his lap and eyed the unopened box. "How did you know what my answer was?" she asked. "Open it."

Ted took off the top of the box and peered inside. "What's this?" he cried.

Molly sat back and waited for him to read her note. Then she explained. "Each cookie's a wish. There are thirteen of them and they're sort of like coupons. You can redeem them from the Molly A. Ramirez Corporation whenever you want."

Ted read some of the wishes: one ride on the scariest roller coaster in the D.C. area, one winter dip in the ocean, one cone of Superchunk chocolate ice cream. Each wish had to do with a special moment he and Molly had shared last summer. Ted put the box down and wrapped his arms around Molly's narrow waist. She reached for his face with her delicate hands and drew his lips toward hers.

Ted held her as if he'd never let her go. Finally, Molly pulled away and smiled into his eyes. "So, are you going to be my date for the Valentine's Dance tomorrow night? Or do I have to find another jock to take me?" she teased.

His answer was another kiss. Molly savored his kiss, and for a moment, she debated telling him the best part of her news. Then she decided it could wait until tomorrow, until Valentine's Day — after the dance. She wanted Ted to know she was with him because she loved him. And only for that reason.

* * *

"Einerson, either you start sharing the girls, or the cookies — that's an ultimatum!" Steve Corbett joked.

Once Woody had left, Bart had come out of the shower. He was trying very hard to ignore the jokes about the cookies, about being voted Mr. Popularity or whatever the pom-pon girls had dubbed him. He was used to being teased about girls, and he usually responded. But today, he wasn't in the mood to hear his buddies' jibes.

"Lay off, Steve!" Bart yelled. "All of you, just lay off." He yanked open his locker and pulled out his clothes.

A sudden uncomfortable silence descended over the locker room. Marc cleared his throat, and the other guys drifted away. Bart sat on a bench to pull on his cowboy boots. Marc sat down next to him.

"What's going on with you, Bart?" he asked. "For the past two days you've been stomping around like a wounded lion."

"Isn't it obvious?" Bart said curtly.

Marc regarded his friend. "No, nothing's obvious. So you got a bunch of silly cookies from those girls who follow you around. What are you so mad about?"

Bart jumped up. He jammed his hands into the pockets of his jeans and strode to the far end of the row of lockers, then back again. He threw his head back and stared at the ceiling. Finally he sat down heavily.

"It's Holly, Marc," he said. "It's over. Everything's gone wrong." After a moment's silence he told Marc the whole story. "When I saw her Monday with Matt . . . that just sort of clinched it."

"Whew — that's intense," Marc commiserated. "But maybe it's not the way you think. Have you asked her what's happening?"

Bart stared at him blankly. "I *saw* what's happening. What's there to ask? I guess I should have met her like we planned. Maybe she would have told me then, but now there doesn't seem to be much point in talking to her."

Marc got up and ran his foot along the row of lockers. "Holly's not like that, Bart. You know that. I'd give her the benefit of the doubt if I were you. You haven't behaved that splendidly yourself," he reminded Bart.

Bart glowered at his friend. "Since I've been dating her, I've never gone out with another girl."

Marc continued to press. "Maybe not, but you come on to every girl you see, Bart. If I did that, Dee would walk out on me in a minute. She'd never stand for it." Marc sat down again. He straddled the bench and faced Bart. "It must be really hard on Holly. Don't you think?"

Bart stared uncomprehendingly at Marc. He was saying exactly what Holly always said. Bart leaned back against the locker to let Marc's words sink in. Holly wasn't just being a typical jealous girl. Slowly he realized he was crazy to think of her like that, and he was ashamed. He was the one who'd been a jerk. He had been lucky enough to meet the most wonderful girl in the world, and sometimes he acted like she didn't even exist. Bart tried to recall the day Holly met Matt at the gas station. How had he behaved? He had watched that blonde climb off her motorcycle; he'd challenged her with his eyes and his smile. Bart didn't have to *go out with her* to be unfaithful to Holly. Acting like that was as good as slapping Holly in the face. Bart froze inside.

Marc thumped Bart on the shoulder. "You okay?" he asked, concerned.

Bart took a deep breath. "I am," Bart answered very slowly. "Suddenly I really *am*." He jumped up, his jaw set. His blue eyes looked determined. Talking to Marc had made everything clear. Bart had to talk to Holly, *now*. He would have to face the music: Either she was seeing Matt or she wasn't. But if she wasn't. . . .

Bart grabbed his coat and books and started for the door. "Uh, Marc . . . thanks." Without turning around he hurried out into the hall.

Chapter 23

"Good-night, Dr. Ellerbee!" Holly called back over her shoulder. Late as usual, she thought, checking the large metal clock over the side door of the medical clinic. She pulled her pea coat from her locker and headed slowly for the door. Why did her four P.M. to eight P.M. shift always end at ten? she wondered. Not that it mattered these days. Without Bart around, her nights were pretty free. Work at the clinic kept her mind off him, at least until her shift was done.

Holly stopped beneath the street light and searched her bag for her car keys. After finding them, she leaned back against the building and gulped down a couple of breaths of cool, fresh air. Now that her shift was done, she could let her guard down. She could cry the whole way home if she liked, then crawl into bed and collapse. For three days now she had barely been able to hold the tears back; ever since Bart had stood her up.

A movement in the shadows on the weedy fringe of the lot caught her eye. Holly felt a sudden rush of fear. She stepped back toward the safety of the clinic entrance, then noticed the familiar boxy shape of a car parked in the far corner. It was a Jeep. Holly blinked and when she opened her eyes again, Bart was coming toward her across the deserted lot. His stride was strong and determined. Just watching him, the tears dried on Holly's face. Her heart started beating faster. She stepped off the curb and very slowly walked forward to meet him.

Holly and Bart met in the middle of the lot. With a few feet between them they stopped. Holly searched his face. It was hard to read his expression in the dark. Bart must have sensed this, because he stepped a little closer, into a pool of light cast by the curbside street lamp. They stood like that, looking at each other for a long moment. And then they were in each other's arms.

"Oh, Bart!" Holly finally whispered in his ear. "I'm so sorry. I have so much to tell you."

"No." Bart pulled away. He placed a finger on her lips. "Not now. It doesn't matter, Holly. It doesn't matter anymore."

Holly looked deep into his eyes and realized that he knew about Matt. She tightened her hold around his neck and he pulled her tightly against him. There was something so fierce and strong about his hug. Holly stepped back and looked at him, her face full of questions.

"I understand," Bart said. "I finally understand what you meant about all those girls. But Holly, I promise, I won't do it again. Ever."

Holly was silent for a moment, but she really did believe him. She knew she didn't have to tell him that when he gently ran his hands along her sides and kissed her in a way that said she was the only one for him.

Chapter
24

"So, what happened to the other sleeve?" Brian Pierson asked, looking at Karen's dress with bright eyes. He pulled his hand out from behind his back and produced a corsage. It was a single big floppy flower, the most brilliant shade of red Karen had ever seen. She thought it was wonderful — almost as wonderful as Brian standing there on her front porch.

"What are you doing here?" she said, knowing exactly why he had come. She looked behind him for Marc and Dee. The only car in the Davis driveway was his electric-blue Trans Am. Even under the low night lights it glowed.

"I told Dee her chauffeur service wasn't needed!" he quipped. "May I come in?" he asked, looking over her shoulder. Karen followed his glance and wheeled around. Her mother was behind them in the hall, still dressed in her suit from work, her briefcase tucked under her arm.

"Sure, of course. I have to get my coat." She mumbled her way through some kind of introduction and left her mother to the mercies of Brian's unending chatter. Upstairs, she closed the door to her room and sank down on the edge of her bed. Her hands were shaking, her knees were weak. "Shock!" she murmured to herself. "The diagnosis is shock!"

She had expected to see Brian tonight eventually — he was going to the Valentine's Day Dance. He couldn't miss it if he wanted. Peter was going to announce the winner of the radio show contest, but they weren't supposed to be going together. What in the world had possessed him to turn up tonight?

She pinched herself to be sure she was awake. Then she spied the corsage in her hand. She walked to the mirror and pinned it on her dress. Karen vaguely remembered that guys were supposed to pin corsages on, but after Brian's comment about her sleeve, she wasn't sure she trusted him; she wasn't in the mood to be stabbed. She grinned at her reflection. In spite of his remark, she knew he liked the way she looked. Karen didn't want to be away from him a moment longer so she turned around and flew down the steps straight into his arms.

On the drive to the gym, he finally began to explain. "So, I surprised you, did I?" He flashed a grin across at her.

Karen arched her delicate eyebrows. "Not exactly," she said.

Brian chuckled. "You know, Karen, you have a very weird way of letting a guy know you like him."

"Talk about weird," she said, having no idea what he meant. She playfully tapped Brian's thigh. He was wearing a suit that looked like it was made out of something that was once very alive. It was weird, but he looked good in it.

Brian turned the car onto a dead-end street and parked. He shifted in his seat to face her. "Karen, I got your message. I was sort of shocked." His face was suddenly serious. The way he looked at her sent a pleasant shiver down her spine.

"My message?" Karen stammered, grabbing the door handle to steady herself.

"On my machine. You called Sunday?" Suddenly he didn't sound so sure of himself. "If someone else was playing a joke — " His voice trailed off and he slicked back his hair. "But it doesn't matter. We're together now and that's what counts, isn't it?"

"Oh, Brian!" Karen reached over and touched his face very gently. "I'm so happy you turned up tonight. And I loved the valentine — and the music Monday during your show." With every word, Brian's face brightened. "But I never left any message. I called Sunday and got your machine, but I didn't see the point of talking to a — " Karen stopped, horrified.

She stared at Brian. "I don't believe this," she murmured after a long silence. "I was too startled by your message. I didn't hang up right away. . . ." Suddenly her face grew hot. She had never been so embarrassed in all her life. Karen couldn't remember exactly what she had said about him to her friends, but the idea that he had heard it. . . . Her words were on his tape.

Brian's hand closed around hers. "Hey, it's okay." He gently ran his finger down her cheek. "I'm really glad. I felt so terrible after Saturday. I should have called you first . . . but I was scared."

After a pause, he continued. "I thought about what you said. You were right, you know — "

"About why you kissed me?" Karen gasped.

Brian rolled his eyes. "You have a one-track mind — did anyone ever tell you that?" Karen shook her head.

He stopped talking long enough to kiss her. Brian finally drew away reluctantly.

"You were right about the contest. It's hard staying friends and having to compete against each other. I wanted to be with you badly, but I also wanted my show to win."

"Me, too," Karen admitted.

"But to tell you the truth, if having my show meant losing you — " Brian got a moony look in his eyes.

Karen sat up straight. She popped him playfully on the nose. "Brian Pierson, you're a liar! You'd take the show and leave me and I'd do the same to you!" she teased.

He didn't say a word. He leaned across the seat and kissed her on the lips. "At least after tonight it'll be over."

"Over?" Karen cried. She grabbed Brian's face and looked deep into his eyes.

"Forget it — we've only just begun!"

He started up the car and they drove the rest of the way to school in laughter.

Chapter
25

"ALL RIGHT OUT THERE, CARDI-
NALS!" Peter Lacey's voice boomed across the
decorated gym. Red balloon hearts hovered in
nets close to the ceiling, and the Sweets to the
Sweet booth had been transformed into a refreshment stand. Red, pink, and white streamers
billowed above the drafty expanse of the basketball court. Spirits were high; the turnout was the
best ever. WKND's fund for running expenses
was replenished for another year. Peter grabbed
the mike and strolled upstage. "The moment
you've all been waiting for has arrived."

Everyone started cheering. Dee and Marc
were right behind Karen. Dee squeezed Karen's
shoulder. Marc bent over and whispered good
luck to Brian. Karen's arm tightened around
Brian's waist. She closed her eyes and made a
fervent wish that however things turned out,
nothing would come between them.

"Our first feature of the evening — " Peter paused dramatically and baited the crowd. "Who can guess?"

"THE RADIO SHOW!" someone shouted.

Peter purposefully shook his head. A gleeful smile crossed his handsome face. "The gentleman in the corner is wrong."

"Get on with it, Lacey!" someone else jeered.

"All right, already!" He shrugged sheepishly, then gestured toward the makeshift wings of the temporary stage. "The time has come for the unveiling — so to speak — of the lovely mystery lady: Candy Hearts!"

The roar that went up in the gym was deafening. Karen covered her ears. Behind her, Woody and Kim groaned loudly in unison.

Jonathan Preston's distinctive voice yelled, "Who are you kidding?"

Peter pretended not to notice. He walked into the wings and returned a second later with his radio star. Although she held an old-fashioned, lacey black eye mask on a stick over her face, Candy Hearts had a very familiar pair of great legs, most of which were showing beneath her red velvet minidress.

"Madame!" Peter bent over in a deep and formal bow. "Reveal yourself, please."

The guys in the crowd hooted and whistled and stomped.

With a very dramatic gesture, Candy Hearts lowered her mask and tossed it into the crowd. The effect was electric. Everyone started laughing and screaming all at once. Laurie Bennington's face lit up as she slithered up to the mike and batted her long dark lashes at the frantic audience.

"Now, everyone." She made a futile gesture to calm them down. "I have one announcement to make before the really big news of the evening breaks. Thanks to your incredible support and to Sasha Jenkins and the staff of *The Red and the Gold*, Candy Hearts is going to return — "

A ripple of conversation buzzed through the gym. "As far as I can see she hasn't left yet," some wise guy yelled from the back.

Laurie pushed her hennaed hair off her face and smiled, pleased. "No, not me. A new and truly anonymous Candy Hearts — in the pages of *The Red and the Gold*. So," she added coyly, "let's give whoever she — or he — might be a warm hand. And thank you all for confiding in me." Laurie's voice had an unmistakably genuine warmth in it. "I really mean that." She blew everyone a kiss and walked off the stage.

Peter approached the mike to make his next announcement. "The turnout at our WKND polls was truly amazing. And I know all four contenders would like to thank you for your support. Even more amazing are the results," Peter said, glancing out over the audience.

Karen took a deep breath. Brian did, too. They looked at each other. "Good luck!" they whispered to each other.

"*Cloaks and Jokes* and *Unicorns and Flugelhorns* came in third and fourth place respectively."

Some disappointed moans and groans rippled across the gym.

"But we have a virtual tie between *What's News* and *Soundings*!"

The commotion greeting Peter's announcement was unbelievable. Karen's hands flew to her face. She couldn't believe it. Her dream was coming true.

She whirled toward Brian. He had his head thrown back, and he was laughing a hearty belly laugh. Karen began laughing, too.

"The question is," Peter continued, "What to do? WKND's advisor and Monica and I talked it over tonight. Of course it's up to the creators of those two worthy shows, but we thought maybe a split-time arrangement would work, or a combination of news and new music would be great. Let's get the lucky winners up here and ask them."

Brian clutched Karen's hand and dragged her toward the stage. Just before they climbed up, he whispered something quickly in her ear. Karen look at him a moment, then nodded vigorously.

Peter beckoned them to the mike. "Who's first?" he asked, his green eyes laughing.

Brian shoved Karen forward. Karen shoved Brian. Finally Brian took the mike in his hand and stepped stage front. His other hand held Karen's. "Well there, Cardinals." His voice rang out. "We're as surprised about this as you are, but happier than you can imagine." He looked warmly at Karen. Everyone cheered. "Karen and I just decided the show won't be shared time. It'll be one show called *Newsnotes*, combining all the news you need to know and the best that is new in music and sounds. So tune in next week for our premiere edition."

Peter took the mike back, and Brian hugged Karen. Then he jumped off the stage and held his arms out. Karen leaped down into his grasp. Just then someone pulled the strings and a blizzard of red and pink heart-shaped balloons cascaded from the ceiling.

"How are we going to do it?" Karen whispered into Brian's ear as the music started up again. It was a slow dreamy song she didn't know.

"Shhh," Brian said, wrapping his arms around her. "Let's dance. We have tomorrow and tomorrow and tomorrow to worry about our show."

Karen had a feeling there weren't quite that many tomorrows before their show had to shape up, but as she and Brian began to move to the music, she suddenly didn't care. Together, she was sure, they could do anything.

Molly surfaced from a long, sweet kiss and nestled her head against Ted's chest. They were sitting behind the bleachers in the gym. Though the speakers were right above them, the loud reggae tune seemed to come from very far off, another world. Tonight, with their arms around each other, Molly and Ted were lost in a world of their own. The only music Molly needed to hear was the beating of Ted's heart beneath his shirt. Listening to that, she felt every cell in her body was dancing.

Molly sighed and propped her elbow on her knee. She leaned over and traced the laugh lines that crinkled the skin around Ted's clear blue eyes. "Shall I read your future?" she asked, faking a gypsy accent.

Ted pretended to consider. "Depends."

Molly pulled back, offended. "On what?"

"What the future is."

Molly's face blossomed into a smile. She sat up straight, practically bumping her head on the bottom of the seat above. "Oh, Ted, I can't tell you anymore," she said. She smoothed the ruffles on her red peasant blouse, and tugged down her skirt.

She grabbed Ted's hand between both of hers and gave it a kiss. "I have some news — some wonderful news." Her dark blue eyes were shining. "Mom's made a decision. We're going to stay here no matter what, even if Georgetown doesn't work out."

Ted leaned forward. He took Molly's chin between his hands and searched her face. "You're serious," he stated. "You're really serious about this."

Molly threw her head back and laughed joyously. "Yes. I mean, she still might get tenure at Georgetown, but the point is she doesn't want me to change schools again next year. My kid sister, either. She's got one more year to go before high school. And I think it's good for Mom, too — after Dad died and all. Home reminds her too much of everything." Molly found those last words difficult.

Ted drew her face toward his and kissed her very gently on the eyes, the lips. Molly wound her arms around his neck and kissed him back.

* * *

After three false starts, Matt pushed himself up the side stairs of the gym and into the dance. He stood in the door and braced himself against the overpowering tide of pulsing music, wildly dancing bodies, and incredible noise. Dances had never been his thing. Matt shifted his shoulders uncomfortably. His dark vintage jacket was too tight, the knot in his tie was wrong, and he felt stiff and weird and out of place. With his right hand he slicked back his dark hair. In his left he held a bunch of violets he'd picked up at the last minute.

Feeling a bit awkward, he held the flowers behind his back and sidled over to a shadowy corner far from the refreshment table. Balloons were floating down from the ceiling. Peter's announcement about the show must have already been made. Matt sighed and checked the clock over the scoreboard. Ten minutes; he'd give himself ten minutes. If Holly didn't show up he'd leave. If she showed up with Bart, well, he wasn't quite sure what he'd do.

Slowly his dark eyes scanned the room. It was hard to make out faces in the flashing lights. But he knew he'd recognize Holly instantly, even if he couldn't see her face. At a table near the front he spotted Jonathan and Fiona. In spite of his churning stomach, Matt smiled. Fiona was wearing something that looked like aluminum foil, but she looked cute cuddling up next to Jonathan. Matt looked away quickly. He didn't want Jonathan to see him there.

Matt looked back toward the door. One moment there was just an anonymous crush of kids, the next moment she was there. Holly wore a golden flower in her hair and a bright yellow dress that swung around her legs gracefully as she hurried across the floor. His heart started pounding in his chest. She was heading straight toward him. Matt stepped out of the shadows and into the whirl of lights. But Holly didn't see him; she hurried by. Matt knew he should leave then, but he stood rooted to the spot, hypnotized. He watched as she began to smile, then threw herself in Bart Einerson's arms.

Matt breathed a sigh. He slipped back to the dark wall. He shouldn't have hoped. He had told himself that last night — Holly had been very honest with him. He shouldn't have come. Matt tugged at his tie and raked his calloused fingers through his hair. Suddenly the crowded gym seemed too hot, too small, too closed in. He kept out of range of the dancers as he headed to the door, eyes on the floor. A high-pitched giggle made him look up. Lined up along the wall, behind the refreshment table, four or five girls were eyeing the crowd. They looked very young and very nervous. Freshmen, he thought to himself, and in spite of the heavy feeling in his chest, he smiled. It was a sad, fleeting smile, and in that moment he ached for them. All they wanted to do was to have some guy ask them to dance. Matt had an impulse to walk over to ask one of them when the next song started. His eyes lighted on a short, chunky girl in a bright, flowered dress. A smile was pasted on her face but she looked like she was close to tears.

He walked up to her and smiled down into her startled pale eyes. But he didn't feel like dancing. Instead, he handed her the rapidly wilting violets and said very tenderly, "For you!"

He turned on his heel and went out the door, feeling a little crazy and very embarrassed. Halfway to his car he stopped and took a deep breath. The cool air cleared his head a little. He thought about how happy Holly had looked in Bart's arms. His breath caught in his throat. He wanted her to be happy, but it hurt. He kicked at a clump of grass and stared forlornly at his boots.

Peter Lacey's voice suddenly rang out across the darkened quad. A cheer went up inside the gym. Matt pulled off his tie and stuffed it in his pocket. He threw his head back and looked up at the stars. Tonight he couldn't find Orion. Holly had told him it was easiest to find in winter. Now spring was almost here. He'd have to try again next year. And he'd find love again. There'd be another girl. Suddenly he was sure of that: Someone out there was made just for him.

Chapter
26

The first few notes of the song were slow and oddly familiar. The lights were dim and Holly felt her body melt into Bart's as they moved together under the lazily flickering strobe lights. Then the lyrics started. It was "Desperado," their song.

"Let's go, Holly," Bart whispered after the song ended. "It's a clear night and there's no moon. Great night for checking out the stars."

Holly didn't answer. She let Bart lead her silently across the crowded dance floor toward the door.

As they stepped out into the cold night air, Holly opened her arms wide and smiled. After the stuffy heat of the dance, the breeze felt delicious against her face, her neck. She felt like she had just walked out of the sun into the shade on a hot summer day. Bart was standing behind her;

his arms circled around her waist, and Holly leaned back against his broad, strong chest. "February's not so bad after all, is it?" she said, closing her hands over Bart's. They stood there quietly, holding each other, swaying slightly in the wind.

Then, hand in hand, they started for the lot where Bart's Jeep was parked. They took the shortcut through the tennis courts. Holly trailed her finger along the green wire fence, thinking of nothing, just feeling the warmth of Bart by her side.

In the middle of the court Bart stopped. He leaned against the fence and drew Holly toward him. "What about the Jeep, the stars, and our ride in the countryside?" she teased, as he ran his hands up the side of her neck and through her hair.

Bart didn't answer. He looked at her very intently before he kissed her. Holly wound her arms around his neck. As they kissed, Bart began to spin her round and round. Holly let her head fall back so she could look up at the stars. They seemed to be swirling in the sky.

Gradually Bart came to a stop. He kept his eyes on hers and said, "I love you, Holly."

"Oh, Bart," Holly cried. "I love you, too."

They sank down together onto the smooth surface of the court. It was cold and damp, but Holly didn't notice. She was watching Bart's face. The parking lot lights played over his rugged features. She delicately ran her finger down the side of his jaw. Bart's lips turned up into the slow, inviting smile that no girl could resist, especially Holly. And now she knew he was smiling it just for her. Just like she knew, as their lips met in a long, slow kiss, the only stars Bart wanted to watch were in her eyes.

Coming Soon . . .
Couples #19
SHOW SOME EMOTION

As Pamela entered the living room, Matt saw her staggering under the weight of the cooler and hurried over. "Let me help," he said, taking the outer edge of the cooler. The unexpected change in weight distribution threw Pamela off balance. Ice cubes skittered over the edge of the plastic cylinder and clattered onto the floor. Some quick footwork saved her from falling, but the cooler tipped the other way when she let go completely and ice and frigid water spilled down Matt's front and splashed down on Pamela's dog, Angie. Matt thrust the cooler back into her hands and jumped back in surprise; Angie yipped and retreated to a corner in the kitchen.

"Here," Matt said. His face was bright red. He slipped his hands under the cooler and took the weight of it from her. For a long, long moment his fingertips touched hers. Pamela thought all the ice would melt with the heat that shot through her from Matt's brief touch. Then he stepped back and carried his awkward burden to the table.

"Poor Matt," Gloria cooed. "You're all wet."

Pamela looked up from the floor and over at them. Gloria was trying to blot the water from Matt's shirt, and he was trying to get her to stop. Suddenly a painful expression took over his face. He finally managed to get Gloria to stop wiping at his chest. He stepped back, reached into his shirt pocket, and pulled out an ice cube. Everyone burst into laughter, and Woody led a round of applause. "What's next?" he called. "A rabbit?"

"No," Pamela said, straightening up. "A towel and a dry shirt. You guys help yourselves to soda. We'll be right back."

"Here," she said, turning on the bathroom light and handing him a towel. She studied his shoulders and chest for a moment. "I'll get one of Dad's shirts. It may be a little small for you but it'll have to do."

"Hey, you don't need to —"

She close the bathroom door on his protest. Her father had half a dozen cotton polo shirts in his drawer. She thought for a minute about Matt's coloring, selected a navy one, and returned to tap on the door. Matt opened it. He was holding the towel in one hand and wearing only his jeans. Wordlessly she handed him the shirt and fled red-faced down the stairs to find Gloria watching her with narrowed eyes.